The motorcycle careered along the mountain highway

Bolan eased up on the throttle slightly, even as he gained ground on the speeding car.

A sharp bend loomed ahead, and the warrior leaned into the turn, guiding the Goldwing with an expert hand.

As the Executioner came out of the curve, a stream of black oil shot from the rear of the limo onto the highway. He swerved to avoid it, but a half second later the bike hit the slick and skidded out of control.

Bolan fought the machine, but it seemed to have a life of its own and headed straight for the cliff.

The Goldwing smashed into the guardrail, the impact hurtling Bolan over the handlebars toward the ground—five hundred feet below.

MACK BOLAN®

The Executioner

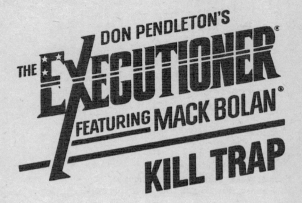

DON PENDLETON'S
THE EXECUTIONER®
FEATURING MACK BOLAN®

KILL TRAP

A GOLD EAGLE BOOK FROM
WORLDWIDE.

TORONTO • NEW YORK • LONDON • PARIS
AMSTERDAM • STOCKHOLM • HAMBURG
ATHENS • MILAN • TOKYO • SYDNEY

First edition June 1990

ISBN 0-373-61138-2

Special thanks and acknowledgment to
Kirk Sanson for his contribution to this work.

Printed in U.S.A.

There is no calamity greater
  than lavish desires.
There is no greater guilt
  than discontentment.
And there is no greater disaster
  than greed.
                    —Lao-tzu
                c. 604—c. 531 B.C.

Every man has to take responsibility for his own
actions—there's no such thing as a free ride. If greed
drives a man to commit treasonous acts, then he has
to face the consequences.

                              —Mack Bolan

THE
MACK BOLAN®
LEGEND

Nothing less than a war could have fashioned the destiny of the man called Mack Bolan. Bolan earned the Executioner title in the jungle hell of Vietnam.

But this soldier also wore another name—Sergeant Mercy. He was so tagged because of the compassion he showed to wounded comrades-in-arms and Vietnamese civilians.

Mack Bolan's second tour of duty ended prematurely when he was given emergency leave to return home and bury his family, victims of the Mob. Then he declared a one-man war against the Mafia.

He confronted the Families head-on from coast to coast, and soon a hope of victory began to appear. But Bolan had broken society's every rule. That same society started gunning for this elusive warrior—to no avail.

So Bolan was offered amnesty to work within the system against terrorism. This time, as an employee of Uncle Sam, Bolan became Colonel John Phoenix. With a command center at Stony Man Farm in Virginia, he and his new allies—Able Team and Phoenix Force—waged relentless war on a new adversary: the KGB.

But when his one true love, April Rose, died at the hands of the Soviet terror machine, Bolan severed all ties with Establishment authority.

Now, after a lengthy lone-wolf struggle and much soul-searching, the Executioner has agreed to enter an ''arm's-length'' alliance with his government once more, reserving the right to pursue personal missions in his Everlasting War.

PROLOGUE

Giant rotors whirled in glittering circles, generating clouds of dust and grit that danced across the tarmac of the Air Force test base.

A spring sun shone surprisingly hot in the Nevada sky, sending rivulets of sweat cascading down the faces of the senior officers, dignitaries and engineers who had assembled for the maiden flight of the prototype of America's newest assault helicopter. Loudspeakers mounted on a refreshment stand blared patriotic martial music.

Built to achieve superiority over the deadly Russian Hind M-24, the helicopter bristled with an arsenal of rocket launchers and machine guns. But the heart of the new metal monster was invisible, buried in sophisticated electronic circuitry, miles of wiring and hundreds of microchips.

In a modern war, designing the largest, fastest and most technologically advanced airplanes and helicopters was only the beginning of the development process. In order to survive in a potential battlefield hell filled with everything from air-to-air missiles to hand-held infantry rocket launchers, electronic warfare and countermeasures gear had to be capable and reliable.

The new helicopter represented the most advanced thinking in electronic control and automation. Weaponry, target acquisition, electronic counter warfare, navigation and communications had been automated to such a high degree that a pilot and copilot could effortlessly operate a behemoth carrying as much firepower as a tank platoon.

Tom Clarkson sipped a cold soft drink and mopped his forehead. As president of Clarkson Industries, he had a major stake in the outcome of today's trial. His firm had designed one of the most critical elements dealing with pilot control systems, leading-edge technology that was partly his personal brainchild. If the flight succeeded, his company would receive tens of millions of dollars in additional defense development contracts.

An Air Force officer gave a short speech from the podium in front of the bleachers, where the guests slowly broiled in the heat.

The brigadier in charge of the demonstration had delayed the takeoff for more than an hour while the technical staff chased down a last-minute glitch that had shown up on the monitors. It had taken some heavy pressure from an embarrassed senior Air Force general to prevent the show from being canceled.

Clarkson sighed with relief as the big bird finally lifted off. The plan for the day was simple—move and hover a few times, concluding with a low-speed attack on a mock-up of a Soviet T-72 tank a half mile from the reviewing stand.

Today's demonstration had been designed only to show members of the Senate and armed forces committees that the billion or so spent on producing the prototype hadn't been wasted. More sophisticated tests would follow by the dozen.

The helicopter moved and halted without incident. Then it began the long sweep to the firing point, Clarkson's throat tightening with anticipation.

Suddenly the bird gave a lurch, its nose dipping unexpectedly. The crowd gasped.

A technician in the background fiddled with his controls, and the pilot's voice, tense but composed, came over the loudspeakers.

"I can't hold it. The controls have gone dead."

Emergency vehicles careered down the airstrip and across the dusty fields toward the stricken aircraft.

"Switch to manual and set it down," the control tower commanded. A mile away, the helicopter spun as though it were a leaf in a breeze.

"Negative. Override inoperative."

Abruptly the assault vehicle heeled over on its side and plunged as the rotors stopped spinning. A fireball erupted from the crash site.

The crowd sat stunned as two men and eight years of work burned on the blistering sand of the Nevada desert.

CLARKSON LOUNGED in the quiet and comfort of his private jet, an oasis from the chaos of the airfield. He knew the screaming and finger-pointing had just begun, and would continue unabated for months to come.

He sat with circuit diagrams, examining possible sources of error. Although the helicopter's black box had yet to be recovered and deciphered to pinpoint the cause of the crash, Clarkson had a horrible feeling that components from his company might be involved.

It was one of the worst days in his life.

But the day wasn't over yet. Clarkson reached for the phone and made a short call before he immersed himself in technical diagrams for the rest of the long flight home to Chicago.

THE OFFICE WAS CLOAKED in darkness except for a narrow oval of light illuminating the papers neatly arranged on a broad cherry desk. A man sat behind the desk puffing on a pipe as he read the material spread out before him. His work was interrupted by a sharp rap at the door.

He quickly put the papers into a black folder and placed it in a drawer. "Come in," he barked.

A young man entered the room and walked to the desk, clicking his heels as he halted. He handed over a short message and left immediately.

The man set aside his pipe and retrieved a small book from a safe. It took only a few minutes to decipher the message with the help of his codebook. At the end he read the full text once more and smiled.

He placed the decoded message into the ashtray and burned it to cinders before he crushed the ashes with the bowl of his pipe.

1

Bolan arrived in Washington two days after Justice Department mandarin Hal Brognola sent out his summons. Where the Executioner had been or what he had been up to, Brognola didn't question. It was enough that his old friend was available to lend a hand. In spite of the many years of their association, Bolan's business was his own, and Brognola respected the limits of their friendship.

The warrior wasn't by any means an employee, official or otherwise. He assisted Brognola when and if the mission the Fed proposed interested him or was something that he would have looked at on his own.

Brognola didn't waste time after a few brief amenities. "Did you hear about the crash of the new attack helicopter prototype?"

Bolan nodded, as Brognola had expected, for very little escaped the warrior's notice. The big man sitting across from Brognola had sources of information, both high and low, that even the CIA envied. Sometimes the word passed through official channels via Justice, but more often it came from a large, loose circle of contacts developed over years of saving other people's bacon.

"Here's something you probably haven't seen." Brognola handed over a file containing the preliminary report of the crash investigation team. "Tell me what it means to you."

The big Fed settled back in his chair, covertly watching the warrior turn the pages back and forth, analyzing and evaluating the data. Bolan didn't have much formal education beyond high school, but the federal anticrime kingpin trusted Bolan's common sense more than an alphabet of fancy degrees.

As Brognola knew, the report, couched in a lot of qualifying statements designed to protect all concerned, concluded that a failure of unknown origin in the automatic control circuitry had caused the crash.

The circuitry had been developed by Clarkson Industries.

"So Clarkson Industries screwed up a design." Bolan tossed the folder back on Brognola's cluttered desk. "What does that have to do with Justice?"

"People make mistakes. That's not news, that's the way it is. But the control circuits Clarkson supplied were supposed to have been tested thoroughly for just the kind of situation that caused the helicopter to crash. Maybe it was simple carelessness on the part of the manufacturer. Maybe it was a lot more serious than that."

"You're talking sabotage, Hal."

"Clarkson had a lot to lose if his new components failed," Brognola continued. "Why would he pass along faulty components?"

Bolan sighed. "Maybe the part burned out under stress, or even was flawed from the beginning. Not every foul-up in America can be traced back to the Russians, you know.''

Brognola laughed wryly. ''Don't I know it. But Clarkson is supposed to be some kind of electronics genius, who still designs most of the company's products. The whole control methodology was his personal idea. If you asked him, he would say it should have worked.''

The big man shrugged, as though to say that Clarkson might simply be a victim of his own ego.

''But there's more,'' Brognola went on. ''A Clarkson employee contacted us to say that he felt there was something funny going on. Nothing definite, but senior employees in key technical positions have been fired and replaced with people not nearly as qualified.''

Bolan sat back, arms folded. ''This seems like a pretty thin patchwork of suspicions.''

Brognola threw up his hands. ''Maybe I'm being overly nervous. The nephew of a friend of mine was killed in the helicopter crash, and it got me thinking. Espionage has become a lot more common than it once was, and the electronics industry is the Russians' prime target. Hell, the Navy picked up a Russian sonobuoy—you familiar with one of those?''

The warrior nodded. He knew it was a device designed to pick up the sounds of propeller rotations and pinpoint enemy submarines. If the other side could find American subs, they could destroy them.

''Well,'' Brognola continued, ''when the Navy took the thing apart, they found that half the circuit boards were stamped 'Made in U.S.A.' If I were a Russian, or even a Brit or a Frenchman for that matter, I'd want to know what was happening at Clarkson Industries.''

Bolan rubbed his chin as he pondered the implications. "You think there are foreign players involved?"

The big Fed shrugged. "I don't know for sure. But Clarkson Industries performs a lot of high-security work. The helicopter that crashed had electronics from Clarkson, as do many other of our most sensitive weapons systems. If I was playing on the other team, it would present an inviting target."

Bolan settled back in his chair with a scowl etched on his face. "You know I'm not a spy, Hal. You've got plenty of spooks to set a trap for the bad guys."

Brognola looked pained at his reaction. "You know the Company isn't allowed to work in the country, at least not officially. And FBI counterintelligence is swamped. They're even more dubious than you are. They claim there isn't enough evidence to justify a look. They've run their security checks, and they're satisfied. I'm not."

Bolan considered the matter. Brognola's skill at separating vital information from a mass of data was nothing short of uncanny. If the man from Justice believed that trouble lurked in the high-tech halls of Clarkson Industries, there was a better than even chance he was on the money.

"Listen, Hal, if I go down to have a look and I find something, I'm not going to try to turn a spy network for you. And I'm not giving the kid-glove treatment to traitors, either."

Brognola grinned at him. "Hell, Striker, why do you think I wanted you for the mission?"

BOLAN ARRIVED at Clarkson Industries in the guise of an Air Force colonel who was to inspect security arrangements. Brognola had made the arrangements on his behalf.

Before he even checked into Clarkson Industries, Bolan contacted Bob Wong, the engineer who had secretly complained about the personnel changes at the company.

Bolan met the man at a quiet bar in suburban Chicago, not far from the Clarkson plant. A balding man in his early forties, Wong impressed Bolan with his levelheaded sincerity. The engineer wasn't an unstable man panicked by shadows, as the warrior had first imagined he might be.

"I don't know what else to tell you," Wong concluded. He had given every scrap of data available under Bolan's quiet probing. "The new men seem all right, if not very sharp technically. But the irregularities worry me. Henry Jaworski and Jimmy Beam, two of the new guys, personally supervised the production of the chips that went into the components in the helicopter that crashed. I'm supposed to be in charge of quality control, which means testing everything that goes out of the plant. But this time I was frozen out completely, not allowed to even touch the stuff." Wong snorted in disgust and drained his beer. He waved the empty mug at a waitress, who hurried over with another round.

"Isn't that a little unusual?" Bolan asked.

"Sure it is! I raised hell about it. I even went to Clarkson himself to complain."

"What did he say?"

"He gave me some nonsense about high security and a rush job and all that. I didn't believe it for a second, but I like my job. What the hell was I supposed to do? Tell the chairman he couldn't run the company the way he wanted?"

Bolan was left with nothing more than his suspicions when Wong left. But an hour's talk with the engineer had set alarm bells ringing in his head. Like Brognola, the warrior was now convinced that trouble lay simmering somewhere below the surface of the respectable high-tech company.

Tom Clarkson had to have reasons for his unusual behavior. The Executioner intended to gather the facts and wring the whole story out of the entrepreneur.

The next day, Bolan drove up to the main gate of Clarkson Industries in a black Lincoln. Clothed in a dress uniform lined with braid and rows of citation markers, he presented a formidable sight to the two gate guards.

He stopped the car at the barrier and flashed a laminated card that bore his picture. "Colonel Rance Pollock, here to conduct a surprise security inspection," he announced to the young security guard.

"Yes, sir," the man replied hastily, and signed to his companion to raise the barrier.

"Just a moment," Bolan ordered, and climbed from the car. "You'd better take a closer look at that identification."

Bolan handed the card to the guard, who looked a little green when he saw that what he had accepted as identification was merely a pass to a Washington health club.

"Do you let in every person with a fancy uniform?" Bolan began as he tore into the hapless guard. He continued in the same scathing vein for another two minutes, finishing with a promise to speak to Clarkson personally about the lax security, before he climbed into the Lincoln and drove off.

Over the next few hours, Bolan made a point of interviewing every employee—and of making himself as unpleasant as possible. With his wide knowledge of security arrangements he had little difficulty in finding fault with every aspect of the operation. He accepted no excuses, no matter how reasonable. From the lowliest employee to the most senior executive, Bolan became an object of intense dislike, which was exactly his objective.

He intended to be as outrageous, irrational, tough and bullying as necessary to flush out anyone with even the least suggestion of a guilty conscience.

But the tactic could backfire—the guilty parties might just sit back and wait for him to leave the complex. But the Executioner thought that scenario less likely than the possibility that he might provoke a violent reaction aimed at silencing him—if he stayed on site long enough.

If he and Brognola were correct about the magnitude of the deception that some Clarkson employees might be concealing, then the opposition wouldn't tolerate any interference with their operation.

If electronic military secrets were being traded, then almost any risk would be worth taking to preserve the flow of sensitive data. The life of one government investigator would be of small consequence to a group of traitors.

Bolan had arranged to present his preliminary findings to Tom Clarkson and several of his key people, expecting that his report might lead to some action. His idea was to turn the screws another few notches, make everyone feel the pressure until something exploded.

In the meantime, Bolan was awaiting an in-depth analysis from Brognola on Clarkson's background, along with that of the key players in the organization. If a traitor was employed by the company, he might be found anywhere—from the mail room to the boardroom.

Too many recent spy cases had made the point that a surprising range of men succumbed to the lure of easy money in return for selling out their country. A good reputation meant nothing—in fact it was required to get the security clearance necessary to have something worth selling.

Everyone was suspect, including Clarkson himself.

The chairman kept Bolan waiting for a half hour past their scheduled appointment time. The big man recognized the cheap power play for what it was. He had lived through too much hellfire to let any kind of corporate intimidation annoy him.

"Listen, Clarkson," Bolan said when he was finally escorted in, "I don't like to be kept waiting. Your silly games certainly won't influence my report to Washington—at least not favorably."

Tom Clarkson, a graying man in his early fifties, sat at the far end of the conference table in an oversize chair that reminded Bolan of a throne. The older man ignored the comment. "Let's hear your report," he snapped. In the course of thirty years, Clarkson had built his business from a basement electronics operation into a prominent defense contracting firm. He had dealt with far more important people than simple colonels, no matter what their mandates. "You have half an hour."

Bolan launched into a review of his findings, stressing possible breaches of security. He spoke without notes for twenty-five minutes.

A dozen men sat around the table, regarding him with a mixture of dislike and a growing sense of unease. As Bolan hammered out fault after fault, the level of tension rose like the mercury in a thermometer placed under a heat lamp.

"I can only conclude," Bolan said, "that security arrangements here are so lax as to represent a significant danger to national security. I will suggest a more detailed study, but I will also recommend that the government suspend all current contracts with Clarkson Industries pending a total revision of security procedures. Get your résumés in order, gentlemen. You're going to be out of a job."

Bolan studied his audience, now reduced for the most part to something close to terrified. These men held highly paid positions, the kind that weren't found in the local want ads.

"Thank you for your interesting comments, Colonel," Clarkson said dryly, stressing the rank. The man was widely regarded as an engineering wizard and had little respect for lesser men. "However, I wouldn't think so highly of your influence if I were you. No one here is going to lose his job because of anything you have to say." He glanced reassuringly at his executives. "I have a great many powerful friends in Washington adept at curbing the pretensions of upstarts. You'll find that out soon enough."

"On the contrary, Clarkson. I have friends even more highly placed than yours. And they know all about your friends—every one of them."

The confident smile left the entrepreneur's lips as his executives began to murmur among themselves. "I don't know what you mean," Clarkson said icily.

"You can't even begin to imagine what I know. I'll be flying back to the Pentagon tomorrow to complete my report. Good luck job hunting, gentlemen. Have a nice day."

Bolan spun on his heel and left, confident that he had planted the seeds of fear where they would do the most good.

Now all he had to do was wait for them to grow.

2

A fistful of death hovered over Mack Bolan's face.

His eyes popped open as he woke suddenly from a sound sleep, alerted by an ever-vigilant combat sense. He thrust a muscular arm from beneath the covers and grabbed the intruder's wrist in an iron grip, shoving it away from his face.

With a grunt of surprise the stealthy assassin dropped the canister he had held. The can bounced off the bed frame and clattered to the floor as the black-suited killer reached for a stiletto with his free hand.

The Executioner threw the bed covers off and lashed out with a foot in a single smooth motion. He released the intruder's arm at the same moment his foot connected with a rock-hard stomach.

The killer stumbled backward and slammed into the wall, rattling the overhead light. The stiletto dropped to the floor.

The warrior jumped from the bed to press his advantage. A faint light shone through the drapes and gleamed faintly on his large, muscular frame.

His adversary reacted quickly. He unsheathed a long knife with a slightly curved blade, and adopted an easy, loose-jointed stance.

Bolan halted just outside the range of the assassin's knife and crouched unarmed, his eyes fixed on the razor edge of the knife. His Beretta 93-R and Desert Eagle lay in a nighttable drawer on the other side of the bed. There was no way to reach them.

The warrior feinted a kick to the groin, but the assassin didn't react. Instead, the man lunged forward and Bolan danced back, narrowly avoiding the thrust.

Bolan grabbed for a lamp on the dresser, intending to hurl it at the killer. It wouldn't budge. A suspicious hotel management had screwed every movable object firmly in place.

The Executioner noted that the connecting door to the adjacent room stood ajar, a small can—probably a lubricant—at its base. That explained the silent, stealthy arrival of the hit man.

Bolan's opponent was a pro. Nearly as tall as the warrior and just as heavily built, he moved with the confidence of a man used to midnight killings. Tight black clothes hugged his body, while a dark ski mask hid his face.

Only the eyes gleamed through, stormy-gray and cold.

Bolan guessed the plan had been to stun him with some sort of knockout gas, then throw his limp body over the balcony to the ground, eighteen floors below. His death would have been written off by the local police as a mysterious accident, or a suicide.

The assassin grinned, his white teeth a beacon in the dark room. He edged forward, the knife aiming to carve a hole in Bolan just below the heart before the big man could maneuver for his gun.

Neither man spoke. The battle continued in silence, broken only by the fighters' adrenaline-charged breathing and the patter of rain on the windows.

Bolan stepped back calmly as the knifer threatened and feinted. The killer played it slow, not taking any chances, knowing that Bolan would run out of space to retreat in a few more steps.

The Executioner motioned as though he planned to rush the other man. His assailant crouched instantly into a defensive posture, poised to impale Bolan as he charged.

The Executioner seized the initiative and grabbed the bedspread heaped at the foot of the bed. Casting it like a net, he enveloped the killer in its pastel folds.

The knifer slashed wildly as the cloth tented over him, the sharp blade tearing wide rents in the flimsy fabric.

Bolan struck, easily avoiding the flailing knife. He grabbed the wrapped figure before the man could extricate himself and hurled him backward with a powerful shove.

The intruder slammed against the curtains that covered the glass doors to the balcony. The draperies parted, and the killer crashed through the doors and landed outside in a heap of torn bedding and shattered glass.

Bolan pounced as the man struggled from under the cloth, minus his knife. He landed a solid punch in the killer's stomach, but the assassin, as big and muscular as Bolan, absorbed the blow easily.

The Executioner wanted to take the guy alive in hope of extracting some information. His opponent had no such intention and aimed a stiff-fingered jab at Bolan's throat, which was designed to crush his larynx.

The Executioner blocked the shot with his forearm and planted one of his own. Instinctively the other man bobbed, but not as successfully. Bolan had aimed to land a blow to the man's chest but connected with his chin instead, sending him rocketing back and over the railing.

Bolan grabbed for the man, but found himself clutching a single shoe and watching the body twist like a high-board diver's until it landed with a soft crunch on the concrete patio below.

BOB WONG HUNCHED LOWER in his seat and adjusted his earphones. He took a last swig of bitter coffee from a plastic foam cup and cast it into a wastebasket with a shudder.

The stuff tasted like paint thinner, and he wondered what damage it was inflicting on his digestive system. His stomach gave a lurch, and he pulled a bottle of antacid from a drawer and swallowed a third of the contents in a single pull. Wong didn't know if the pain was caused by the stress of the job or the abysmal food.

His eyes peered narrowly at the computer console in front of him, watching as numbers marched and jumped as he stroked the keys at his fingertips. To his left, a monitor showed the space shuttle *Galileo*, the latest and most sophisticated addition to the space fleet, ready for launch on the pad. A soft voice in his earphones gave the countdown, currently holding at T minus one minute and ten seconds.

He called up a diagnostic display and retrieved the error, which indicated a loose seal in the cargo bay. Since it posed no threat, he overrode the hold and the countdown resumed.

Tension mounted inversely with the falling countdown.

At T minus thirty seconds, the engines ignited. Power climbed slowly to the titanic levels required to hurl tons of metal and seven crewmen into orbit. Smoke from the Atlas thrusters boiled around the base of the tower, obscuring the giant rocket and its fragile passengers.

Ten, nine, eight, seven... The numbers dropped steadily until the final blast-off when the missile bolted skyward, rotating gradually onto its back as it curved over the Atlantic.

Ten seconds before *Galileo* separated, Wong's panel went haywire as readings flashed danger red. Two seconds later the multibillion dollar spacecraft disappeared in a volcanic blast, sending shards of hot, fused metal cascading into the ocean for a radius of fifty miles.

"Son of a bitch," Wong said breathlessly. He punched a key to invoke the evaluation program and ran through the last few minutes of the *Galileo* flight, pausing every few steps of the program to switch to alternate displays that expanded the details.

"Thank God it was only a test," he murmured. Wong had stayed late to run the final preacceptance test on several pieces of electronic hardware that

Clarkson Industries supplied to the new shuttle. He used a powerful software simulator, which cost almost as much to develop as the spacecraft it represented. By entering the characteristics of the components his company supplied, Wong could verify how the entire system would function without actually having a shuttle to play with.

The computer did all the work of simulating the flight. Sometimes it threw in a curve, placing unexpected stresses on the components, just so the contractors could see what would happen.

Wong had just seen a doozer of an unexpected problem.

He scanned the console, searching for the root of the problem. There shouldn't have been any surprises at this stage. His subordinates had checked out every circuit and condition, several times, under every reasonable circumstance.

At least that was what he'd been told and what the test logs had indicated.

Fortunately Wong had never lost the urge to tinker, and the appeal of the expensive government computer toy had been impossible to resist.

His features settled into a tight frown. His boss wouldn't be happy if a glitch turned up at this late date. In a few weeks the components were scheduled for delivery. If they missed the deadline, NASA would scream, particularly since Clarkson had run far over budget already.

Wong verified that the characteristics of the components had been entered correctly. They had.

As far as he could tell, the computer had thrown in a random variation in air temperature at that altitude. One of the components that Clarkson supplied regulated the fuel flow to the shuttle thrusters. Apparently it had been unable to cope with the rapidly changing conditions. Too much fuel had gone into the high-pressure mix. The result: one very expensive fireball and posthumous medals for every crewman aboard.

He ran the test twice more, specifying no changes in conditions.

Two more destroyed shuttles blazed from the simulated monitor.

Wong sighed and keyed the console. A printer erupted into life, creating a recorded trace of the events of the last moments of the shuttle, together with an analysis of the critical factors.

The shuttle could not be launched with the components Clarkson supplied. It would amount to signing the death warrants for the astronauts. After the previous failures of the space program, one more disaster would probably mean NASA would be dead as well.

Wong dialed the number the man from Justice had given him in case of emergencies. Considering the recent helicopter disaster, he thought tonight's test qualified. A problem at this late stage smacked of deliberate error. Routine testing should have caught the bug long ago.

The phone buzzed endlessly, unanswered.

A glance at his watch told him that his boss, the vice president in charge of research, might not have gone to bed yet. The man was notorious for his energy and his attraction for the opposite sex.

Even if Les Anderson wasn't awake, this couldn't wait.

Besides, Wong preferred to discuss the situation away from the prying eyes of the rest of the research staff. Something was very wrong, and he couldn't take any chances until he knew exactly what he was dealing with. For that matter, he just wanted to pass the buck to higher management and wash his hands of the entire matter. This was way out of his league, and he didn't want to get caught in whatever fallout resulted from his discovery.

And he had no doubt that there would be fallout—plenty of it.

There should have been no way that an error of this magnitude could slip through undetected. Either incredible negligence, criminal ineptitude or conspiracy had brought the project to this sorry state.

A strict methodology governed how components were tested before being approved and shipped. Every detail of the final tests was recorded to prevent slip-ups—at least, that was how the system was supposed to work.

On impulse, Wong moved to a high bank of filing cabinets, which contained the printouts of every acceptance test performed at Clarkson. A few minutes of patient searching retrieved the one that he was interested in.

He scanned the computer logs, flipping through the closely printed pages until a single line leaped from the page. The technician who had performed the test had overridden one of the conditions, artificially bypassing the problem that would cause the shuttle to be destroyed.

Someone had known exactly how to suppress any evidence of failure.

Every test required signatures from both the technician performing the test and a supervisor. Wong glanced at the title page. Two signatures occupied the correct positions, but trailed across the paper in illegible scrawls. He doubted that anyone could possibly decipher the names, if they actually represented the names of employees.

The testing department under his supervision had a staff of more than twenty. Any one of them—correction, any two—could be involved in a conspiracy to destroy the reputation of the company and cause untold havoc in the space program.

Bob Wong intended to get to the cause of the problem, starting tonight. He dialed Les Anderson and waited impatiently for the connection.

"Hello?" Anderson answered in a husky voice.

"Les, this is Bob Wong. I've run into a major problem down at the shop. I need to see you tonight."

Anderson swore vehemently. "Can't it wait until morning?"

Wong heard a woman's voice in the background. She was urging Anderson to get off the phone. A glass clinked. After the long day he had spent working, Wong felt no regret at intruding on his boss's love life.

"Afraid not, Les," he replied. "I think we're neck deep in shit and sinking fast. There's something fishy about the quality-control and test procedures being run around here. If this gets out we can both kiss our jobs goodbye. Walls have ears, and so does Ted Michaels.''

Michaels was a colleague who didn't bother to conceal his interest in Anderson's job. Wong might be only a simple Ph.D. in electrical engineering, unused to the finer points of corporate political gang wars, but he had picked up enough dope on his ambitious, unintelligent boss to know the right buttons to push.

"All right. Meet me here at my place in one hour." Anderson clicked off hastily.

Wong held the dead phone for a moment and smiled bitterly. If Anderson thought his pleasant evening romp had been upset, he had better prepare himself for a real shock.

A BLUE PANEL VAN PARKED on a quiet city street attracted no attention among the thousands of other vehicles on the roads. The van's occupant knew this, and had transformed the crowded space into a comfortable home away from home. As long as he changed parking locations regularly, there seemed little prospect that his snoozing and games of solitaire would be interrupted. It had been a pleasant assignment, if tedious.

He sat before a large control panel, surrounded by relays and tape recorders capable of recording fifteen different phone conversations at once. He had nearly finished yesterday's crossword puzzle, aided by an occasional peek at the answers in today's paper.

A monitor light glowed in the dark and a recorder snapped into motion. The technician flipped a switch and listened in. "'Walls have ears,'" he snorted. "Buddy, you don't know the half of it."

A red sticker under the monitor light reminded him that this call involved one of several numbers marked for special attention. According to his instructions, he phoned a local number and relayed the message he had intercepted.

The technician had become an expert at electronic surveillance, thanks in part to a very expensive and thorough education in the military. He had combined his training with flexible ethics to carve a cozy and lucrative little niche in the business world. He figured that he had more wiretaps going in the city tonight than the Feds and the local police combined. Of course they weren't telling, and neither was he.

A secret of success in his business was a remarkable lack of curiosity. He had no idea whose phone he had tapped into, nor did he have any clue as to the identities of the men he transmitted his information to.

He knew better than to ask questions.

Curiosity killed the cat—and there was no coming back.

BOB WONG WALKED into the parking lot, nearly deserted except for the cars of the cleaning staff. He'd been closing the shop a lot lately while he searched for answers concerning the fiery fate of the prototype helicopter.

When he had been a young engineer, he would rather have designed and tinkered than anything else.

Sleep came when necessity drove his weary body into a corner, unable to stand any longer. Many nights he had slept under his desk. He didn't see that kind of dedication from his young staff, who seemed to have an eye on the main chance, out to grab all the salary and perks they could squeeze from the organization, before bolting to the first company that sweetened the deal.

What the hell had happened to the youth of today?

Wong placed the papers he had brought as evidence on the passenger seat. He drove his Buick through the security post with a friendly wave to the night guards and pulled onto the interstate.

A few cars passed him, but traffic thinned as he neared the turnoff to Anderson's home, situated in a remote country area in a belt of farmland. He steered off the highway around a cloverleaf leading into dairy country.

Just after the turnoff he slowed as a young woman waved a flare at him. She stood beside a black Jaguar sedan with the hood up. Even in the harsh glare of the headlights, Wong could see that the woman, tall and Nordic, was remarkably pretty. A light breeze fluffed her blond hair in front of her face in shimmering wisps. A white dress curved around a lean body.

"Can I help?" Wong asked as he pulled up behind her and powered down his window.

"There's something wrong, but I don't know anything about cars." The woman leaned into his window and smiled shyly. One hand played with a golden tau cross dangling from a short chain at her neck. "Could you please have a look?"

Wong stepped from his car and moved toward the black sedan. The blonde fell in behind him, topping him by a good three inches.

The engineer never suspected the judo chop to the neck that felled him.

The woman caught his limp form before he hit the ground. Years of weight lifting enabled her to carry the smaller man back to his car with barely an effort. She leaned him against the fender as she drew on a pair of thin gloves and opened the driver's door, then eased him behind the wheel.

She picked up the printouts from the passenger seat for later disposal and ran back to her car with them. She lowered the Jaguar's hood so no one else would stop to offer assistance, then took from the car a partially consumed bottle of whiskey.

The blonde returned to Wong's car and carefully inserted a thin tube in his mouth and down his throat, since the unconscious man could not swallow. A third of the contents of the bottle disappeared down his throat through the tube. She then capped the whiskey and wrapped Wong's limp hands around the bottle several times before she allowed it to drop to the floor. Fingerprints would identify the bottle as Wong's.

Now she had to exercise a little patience; a coroner would be able to tell the difference between liquor poured into Wong's stomach after death and drunk while he lived. She waited as long as she dared, nearly twenty minutes, to give some of the whiskey time to be absorbed into the stunned man's bloodstream.

Bob Wong's ''accident'' didn't have to be foolproof, just reasonably convincing. Since more than one in three traffic accidents involved alcohol, she expected that the overworked and understaffed rural police wouldn't look very far into another routine road fatality.

Her eyes scanned the road. Each time a car came down the lonely road, she stuck her head into Wong's window as though deep in conversation. The message should be clear to any Good Samaritan inclined to stop: no help needed, thank you very much.

When the road remained dark, with no sign of approaching headlights, the blonde started the car and placed Wong's foot on the accelerator. Reaching through the open window, she slipped the automatic into gear and the car lurched forward. She trotted beside it with one hand on the wheel and steered the moving Buick around her own parked vehicle.

Once the car was on the bridge, a quick turn of the wheel sent it crashing through the flimsy guardrail. The Buick teetered momentarily as the front wheels spun, then toppled in a front somersault into the dark water twenty feet below. The water rushed in through the open window as the car floated for a few seconds before sinking.

The hired killer didn't have time to linger. She jumped into her Jaguar and drove off with a squeal of tires, anxious to leave the crash scene well behind her.

Another appointment with death waited down the road.

Unlike most professionals, she made house calls.

TWENTY MINUTES LATER, Les Anderson opened the door and stood gaping at the lovely blonde on his doorstep. "Yes, can I help you?"

The beauty grabbed his face in her strong, gloved hands and kissed him hard on the mouth. "Bob got stuck with car trouble. He sent me here to keep you company until he arrives. Are you going to let me in?" She arched one perfect eyebrow.

Anderson noted the low-cut dress, revealing the softly rounded shape of firm pale breasts. He stood wordlessly away from the door.

The blonde entered the house and, swaying gently, walked up the stairs. "Is this the way to the bedroom?" she asked from the top.

Anderson nodded. "Who the hell are you?" he asked, puzzled. "What are you doing here?" Wong had surprised and annoyed him with his late-night demand for a meeting. The beautiful visitor represented an unexpected development in an already strange situation.

He wondered briefly if this was some kind of plot concocted to deprive him of his senior position. Wong had always resented his success, he thought.

The young woman laughed softly. "Call me Diana," she replied in a low, melodic voice. "If you come up and keep me company, I'll show you exactly why I'm here."

Anderson hesitated, then began to walk toward her.

She waited for him on the top step. When Anderson came within touching distance, Diana spread her arms and reached out as though to hug him.

Instead, the arms shot forward violently, shoving hard into his chest.

Anderson toppled backward with a strangled yell that suddenly choked off as he landed on his head. The vice president rolled, limbs flailing wildly, until he rested in a tangled heap at the bottom of the stairs.

The woman paused for a moment, listening. Her instructions indicated there might be a third party in the house, who would have to be eliminated. Her orders agreed with her own methods. She didn't plan to leave witnesses.

She eased down the steps and felt for Anderson's pulse. A small mirror extracted from her purse and held in front of the man's lips remained clear, confirming that breathing had ceased.

Another household accident, she thought. Poor bugger slips at the top of the stairs and breaks his neck. An open-and-shut case.

The blonde drew a short-barreled pistol from her purse and checked through the house. It proved empty. She sighed contentedly. An additional body to be disposed of would have been just another headache. A quick glance at her watch showed that she had plenty of time to catch a late night flight back to New York, where she could disappear into one of her many identities.

When she left, the hit woman carefully locked the door.

A perfect crime lay behind her and a fat paycheck ahead. As she drove toward the airport, Diana smiled at herself in the rearview mirror. Her professional pride permitted her a moment of self-congratulation.

After all, she had shown again that she remained one of the elite of crime, the best of the hired killers.

Have gun, will travel.

3

Bolan barged past a startled executive secretary and slammed Clarkson's oak door back against the wall. The industrialist and another man, seated at a small conference table, looked up in astonishment.

"Out!" Clarkson ordered after a second, gesturing to his subordinate.

"Don't bother," the warrior said. "This will only take a second. I just wanted you to see that I'm still very much alive and as mean as ever. I've decided to stick around and investigate you and your company personally. I'm going to make your life a living hell from now on."

"I don't know what you mean," Clarkson said coolly, a muscle twitching in his cheek.

Bolan arched an eyebrow, scorn written on his face. "You didn't know that someone tried to punch my ticket last night? I had a caller at my hotel room, a killer who thought I might take a dive off the balcony with a little urging. It's funny what goes on in the vicinity of Clarkson Industries."

The company chairman took a slow sip of coffee from a china cup next to his elbow. "This is all news to me," he replied calmly.

"You seriously expect me to believe that it was simple coincidence that the day I announce that I'll deliver an unfavorable report to my superior in Washington, a hit man tries to murder me?" Bolan snorted in disgust. "I don't believe in coincidences, not that kind."

The industrialist shrugged. "Believe what you like."

Clarkson retained his composure through the exchange, but Bolan was certain that he read more than bewilderment in the man's eyes. If the industrialist hadn't ordered the hit, chances were good that he knew who *was* behind the assassination attempt.

"Well, here's something else—I'm not going back to Washington until I've gotten to the bottom of this nightmare. You can count on it." The big man stormed from the room.

Another twist of the band had tightened around Clarkson's head. Bolan could almost hear it starting to crack.

DARKNESS HAD FALLEN hours earlier.

Bolan had been sitting in his car since before dusk, waiting for Clarkson to make his move. He poured another cup of coffee from his thermos and shifted position to ease his stiffening back. For company he had the entrepreneur's file, as well as dossiers on a dozen other key personnel.

The time had passed quickly as he scanned the records searching for the unusual. For the most part, nothing differentiated the Clarkson employees from any other group of executives. A little tax evasion, a few hidden mistresses, the occasional drinking problem—standard stuff.

Even Clarkson seemed perfectly clean. He'd started his business thirty years ago in a small way and had built it through sheer genius and hard work. He'd been married to the same woman for more than twenty years. His two children were away at college.

Tom Clarkson represented the fulfillment of the American dream, one of the best and brightest. The only red flag on his record concerned numerous large withdrawals from his bank accounts, with no sign of where the money was going. Over the past while, the size and frequency of these withdrawals had increased. Clarkson was spending a hundred thousand dollars a week on average, all unaccounted for.

Even for a man as rich as Clarkson that amounted to a large capital drain. Combined with a few business reverses, the leakage had become a serious hemorrhage.

Bolan guessed it represented blackmail or losses on illegal activities.

The warrior planned to find out this evening. He'd placed a homing device under the bumper of Clarkson's limousine. A little patience might yield some interesting results.

Bolan had spent part of the evening reviewing two grimmer files—the police reports on the deaths of Bob Wong and Les Anderson.

Earlier in the day he had examined the sites of both "accidents." The police files only reinforced the impression he had received at the scenes of the crimes.

Nothing in the evidence contradicted the conclusion that both men had died in accidents. But Bolan didn't believe it for a second.

Bob Wong hadn't struck him as the kind of man to drink himself into insensibility and then drive off a bridge. It occurred to Bolan that he was likely on his way to meet Anderson, who had happened to fall to his death only a couple of miles from where Wong had drowned.

The two deaths created a flimsy tissue of coincidence that rang alarm bells in Bolan's head. Wong and Anderson had been murdered. No doubt existed in his mind on that score.

He hadn't known Anderson, but Wong had seemed a decent man dedicated to his job and anxious to do his part in rooting out whatever evil lurked at Clarkson Industries. Obviously he had stumbled onto some new fact, something that had led to his death, as well as that of the man he intended to meet.

Bolan couldn't help but wonder if the two men would be alive now if only Wong had sat tight until he could speak with Bolan.

The big man knew that "what if" scenarios didn't bring back the dead. In any case, it hardly mattered now.

The homing device gave a faint beep as the Executioner's quarry rumbled into motion. Bolan switched on his own rental vehicle and waited for the stretch limo to nose into traffic.

He followed at a safe distance, keeping a dozen or so cars between himself and Clarkson. With the tracker to ensure that his target didn't escape surveillance, he needn't risk tipping off his quarry by following too close.

The industrialist might be heading for a rendezvous, somewhere to spend a little of his free-flowing cash. On the other hand, he might be planning nothing more sinister than dinner with friends.

Bolan lacked clues. The hit man was a dead end. A search of his body had failed to turn up any identification, not so much as a driver's license. Even the labels in his clothes had been removed. The dead man's fingerprints hadn't matched anything in the Stony Man files. So far, he remained just another unidentified John Doe on a slab in a drawer at the county morgue.

The warrior's usual modus operandi was to hit hard and fast, but his hellfire would have to wait until he found the proper target.

Clarkson headed for the suburbs and continued right through into open country. Bolan dropped back until the limo was out of sight, guiding himself by means of the colored blip wavering on the tracker display.

Finally Clarkson made a ninety-degree turn up ahead, and Bolan slowed to a stop as he approached the point where the limo had left the main road. A cracked asphalt lane led into the tree line, and almost immediately made a sharp turn.

The tracker told Bolan that Clarkson's vehicle had come to a halt about a mile away. The warrior drove a short distance along the lane until he found a spot where he could pull off the road and conceal his car.

Bolan began his recon by fading into the woods, alert for any guards who might be watching the road. If he encountered trouble, his silenced Beretta 93-R hung in its custom webbing under his left armpit. He also toted a camera with a long zoom lens and several rolls of fast film.

He crept silently through the trees parelleling the lane. About a half mile along he passed a checkpoint where two hulking men stood in the middle of the road. Two other guards crouched among the pines, covering the access with leveled AR-15 assault rifles.

The hidden watchers confirmed Bolan's assumption that Clarkson hadn't driven so far into the sticks just to visit a girlfriend.

The warrior passed the hardmen, unseen and unheard, no more than a whisper on the wind. He eased through the underbrush until he arrived at a broad clearing. An A-frame log cabin stood centered among the surrounding trees, and five limos and a large sedan were parked in front of the hideaway. The drivers stood smoking and chatting quietly, but a half dozen men covered all entrances to the building.

None of them carried guns openly, but Bolan would have bet his life that every man was packing.

He circled the house slowly, confident that his blacksuit would protect him from wary eyes. Both front and rear entrances were closely observed, and he doubted that he could reach a side window without being spotted. Heavy draperies prevented anyone from spying on the meeting in progress.

It would be impossible for him to gain entry without knocking out some of the surrounding defenders, which could tip his hand earlier than he intended. He had come to gain information, not to let Clarkson and his secret associates know that someone was dogging their heels. Plenty of opportunity existed for the big man to deal out justice on his own schedule.

He snapped several photographs of the license plates of the cars. The information might prove useful later. Then he settled down across from the entrance to wait. Sooner or later the participants would leave and Bolan would capture their faces on film.

CLARKSON DIDN'T LIKE the cards he was being dealt. He sat back feeling a little sick, as Tony D'Angelo scooped up a large pile of chips. Most of them had once belonged to Clarkson.

Four queens stared at him, his best hand of the night. He had bet aggressively on their promise, thinking that his opportunity to recoup his losses had finally materialized.

Until D'Angelo laid down a straight flush and swept away his hopes.

Not for the first time, the thought formed in his mind that the little Italian might be cheating. D'Angelo usually came out a winner, or lost only a fractional amount. The other players, wealthy businessmen like Clarkson, never seemed to do as well, at least not over the long run.

He would never dare voice his suspicion, not to a volcano-tempered man with a reputation like D'Angelo's.

Clarkson kicked in a white chip for the ante. Using the cheap plastic tokens made it easier to believe that the poker game was only for fun, a little innocent amusement on a night out with the boys.

He called over the chip girl, a bosomy six-foot blonde with a low-cut dress. "Thirty," he said succinctly. She came back a minute later with thirty thousand in chips: ten white chips at a thousand each and ten red ones for double the amount. She bent low enough to give him a good view of her cleavage as she handed over the plastic and a chit to sign.

Clarkson ignored the woman. At these stakes he couldn't afford to be distracted.

The game broke up at midnight according to the time limit the players had set. The engineer grumbled to himself. He had won the last three hands, and just as his luck had finally changed, the end of the match had arrived. It hardly seemed fair.

Gloom swept over Clarkson as a quick calculation showed that he had ended the night $107,000 in the hole. His fingers trembled a little as he wrote the check for D'Angelo. Every week he came expecting to recoup his losses. His gambling urge remained eternally optimistic, convinced, as he was, that it was only a matter of time before lady luck would sit on his shoulder and the tide would turn. He had struck it rich occasionally in the past, once to the tune of more than two hundred thousand dollars. But not this time.

"Listen, Tony, we've got to talk," Clarkson began as the others filed out the door to the waiting cars.

"So spill it," D'Angelo said over his shoulder as he counted his night's receipts.

Clarkson hesitated momentarily before he broached the subject that had occupied his mind all day. Although D'Angelo stood six inches shorter than the industrialist, Clarkson forgot the difference in size when he looked into the other man's cold, pale gray eyes. They revealed absolutely nothing—not warmth, not anger. The searching, unblinking orbs gave Clarkson the feeling that D'Angelo knew every thought he had ever conceived. The little fellow usually acted like an animated statue, although when provoked he might explode into a boiling rage.

"Colonel Pollock, the one who's been investigating security, threatened me today." Even as he spoke, Clarkson wondered how he had let this mental midget, someone so inferior to himself, attain such a position of dominance in his life.

"He believes," Clarkson continued, "that I was behind an attempt to murder him. I think he could make a lot of trouble for me, and that means problems for us."

D'Angelo didn't react for a moment. He just stared Clarkson down, holding the entrepreneur with his glance. "I told you not to worry, didn't I? I said I would take care of problems, and I will. I don't plan to let some Pentagon desk jockey interfere with my business."

"But what are you going to do?" Clarkson persisted, reaching out a hand to grab D'Angelo by the shoulder. "He says he can ruin me, and he doesn't seem like the kind of guy to blow smoke. I take him very seriously."

D'Angelo glared at his companion's hand until the industrialist hastily removed it. "I don't like to be touched," he said in a manner that suggested he just might cut off the offending hand next time. "As for Pollock, leave him to me." He turned away to gloat silently over his poker profits, dismissing the industrialist.

"I want to know what you'll do. I could lose my company," Clarkson shouted at his back. A large part of him didn't care what D'Angelo did as long as the trouble disappeared. But Pollock had appeared quite confident that he could shut down Clarkson Industries.

"All right," D'Angelo said casually. "I'm going to kill Pollock just the way I wasted Wong and Anderson. I tried to hit him last night, but my man failed. Next time I'll succeed."

Clarkson slumped into a chair. He didn't know why he was surprised by the revelation. Actually he had half expected the news, and was instantly sorry he had asked. The admission made him an accessory after the fact to murder, and if Pollock died he'd be implicated there as well.

Now D'Angelo had yet another hammer to hold over his head, another threat to keep him in line.

"Don't get soft on me now, Tom. You just keep your mouth firmly shut and nothing will happen. Otherwise . . . accidents happen."

D'Angelo spoke conversationally, as though murder were an everyday occurrence. In the mobster's world it might very well be the kind of thing he did as casually as throwing out the garbage.

"You need me, D'Angelo," he protested weakly.

"Maybe, maybe not. Don't get stupid on me and start thinking you're indispensable. That would be a big mistake, possibly a fatal one. Now go home and stop worrying."

Clarkson stumbled out of the cabin in a daze. He would have to trust D'Angelo, like it or not. Clarkson knew he wouldn't live out another day if the little shark thought that he might be in danger. He imagined that a squealer could expect no mercy from the deadly thug.

The only certainty in Clarkson's crumbling world was that he had traveled too far along the road to a prison cell to turn back now.

Inside the cabin, D'Angelo had reached the same conclusion. Clarkson was scared, all right. The only trick was to make sure that the industrialist feared him more than anything else.

"Hey, Mario," he called. A slim young man hurried over. "Tomorrow you'll start work for Clarkson as his new executive assistant. I'll call him and let him know you're coming."

"But Tony, I don't know anything about being an executive," his subordinate protested.

"Mario," D'Angelo said, reaching up and patting him on the cheek. "You've only got to know one thing—if you even suspect Clarkson's going to cross me, waste him. Just make sure the body is never found. Got it?"

The young hood grinned. "I got it, Tony."

A few minutes later, D'Angelo dialed Clarkson's mobile phone. The company chairman took the news quietly, as though he'd been expecting it. D'Angelo didn't anticipate any trouble from the cowed man, but he had built his empire through preparing for every eventuality.

Almost the second he replaced the receiver it buzzed furiously. An unpleasant and unexpected voice drifted over the telephone.

"Two murders were something I could overlook," the caller said, "stupid as they were. But your latest botched attempt represents a tremendous nuisance to all of us."

D'Angelo had no intention of accepting criticism from anyone, least of all this man. "I deal with problems my own way. How I do it is none of your business as long as you get what you've paid for. I've always delivered exactly what I've promised, or even better, haven't I?"

"Granted. Keep it that way. Solve your little problem, or we'll eliminate it for you. And that will cost you."

The line went dead.

D'Angelo swore viciously and dropped the phone. He hated dealing with excitable foreigners, especially mysterious ones.

BOLAN SNAPPED AWAY as figures emerged onto the brightly lit porch. Other than Clarkson, the men were strangers. Possibly Brognola would be able to identify them when the information was transmitted back to the command center at Stony Man Farm.

Clarkson looked drawn and shaken as he climbed into his car. Whatever had transpired in the cabin hadn't helped his peace of mind. If, as Bolan suspected, some high-stakes gambling had occurred, Clarkson must have been victimized once again.

However, the last man to step through the cabin doorway proved an interesting surprise. Bolan had known Tony D'Angelo more than a decade ago, when the man was merely an ambitious underboss. Several years ago he had taken control of the local Mafia Family, finally having clawed his way to power.

Since then, D'Angelo's Family had maintained a low profile, involving itself heavily in legitimate business while skirting the areas under high scrutiny by the authorities.

D'Angelo's wealth and power had increased, but he had avoided the attention of the Executioner, who dealt with higher priorities on his hit list. Bookmaking, loan-sharking and prostitution accounted for a fair portion of the mobster's profits, but those traditional vices appeared mild when compared to many of the horrific schemes Bolan had defeated over the years.

Not that that excused D'Angelo in any way. Now that Bolan had discovered that the little gangster was the bug under the Clarkson rock, it was his turn to be squashed. D'Angelo more than deserved it.

However, his retribution would have to wait temporarily.

The pieces of the puzzle didn't fit yet. What was the connection between Clarkson and D'Angelo? And what was Clarkson Industries involved in that had caused the murder of two employees and a hit on Bolan?

The Executioner didn't know, but nothing would stop him from finding out.

4

Bolan wanted answers to the multitude of questions that were piling up like cars in a freeway accident. He had decided that the best way to get them would be to speak to Clarkson one to one. He'd considered waiting until morning and presenting the entrepreneur with photographic evidence of the meeting with D'Angelo. But he doubted that sort of persuasion would prove very effective.

Clarkson was tough and certainly smart, as Bolan expected the founder of a major corporation would be. If the warrior confronted Clarkson in his office, a place where the executive felt comfortable, he doubted that he would admit to anything.

But a surprise visit to his residence might give Bolan the psychological advantage he required to demolish Clarkson's cool veneer.

The big man checked his watch. The luminous dial glowed faintly, dwarfed by the shine of the sliver of moon riding overhead. Three o'clock in the morning. Perfect.

Bolan padded over the businessman's lawn. The house was spacious, but not ostentatiously so, neither the largest nor smallest in the upper-class enclave.

Clarkson obviously had other, more important uses for his limited funds.

The warrior had learned that the industrialist's wife was out of town until the next day, so much the better for what Bolan had in mind. There wouldn't be any noncombatants to complicate matters.

Clarkson placed his faith in security systems, but a lifetime of experience had taught Bolan their limitations. He disabled the alarm circuits within minutes and eased through the back door seconds later.

He stepped softly on the plush carpet of the hall, looking for Clarkson. His search took him to the second story of the mansion, where snores from a bedroom at the far end of the hall guided him along.

The warrior stood at the foot of the bed, a black shadow in a dark room, holding cold steel trained on the sleeping man. He tapped Clarkson heavily on the foot.

The older man woke with a muffled shriek, repeating the scream when he saw the black figure covering him with a gun. "Don't shoot," he pleaded. "Take anything you want, but don't kill me."

"I don't want your money," Bolan growled. "I want information."

"You!" Clarkson gasped in astonishment as he recognized the voice. He sat up in bed. "What the hell are you doing here? Get out before I call the police."

Bolan shrugged. "I don't think so, Clarkson. Tell me about your involvement with Tony D'Angelo."

"You have no right to question me," the industrialist said with an attempt at bravado. "Besides, I don't know what you're talking about."

The warrior triggered a silenced shot, smashing the bedside telephone into fragments. "Wrong answer. I have photographs of you both leaving a cabin in the woods."

"You're no Air Force colonel," Clarkson accused as he came fully awake with a start. "Are you from the CIA?"

Bolan shot again, smashing a mirror on a side wall into a hundred glittering shards of glass.

Clarkson flinched. "All right. I do know him. We play poker together on Friday nights, along with a number of other highly respectable businessmen. That's all."

Another round destroyed a lamp beside the wrecked phone.

"So we do a little business together! There's nothing illegal about that, is there?"

Bolan answered by shooting a picture over the bed. Glass fragments rained down on the cowering executive.

"What the hell are you doing?" Clarkson demanded. This time he was angry. "That's a Chagall print."

"Not anymore," Bolan said dryly. "Keep talking, or I keep shooting."

Clarkson looked warily at his unwelcome visitor, trying to guess how little he could get away with telling. "He got me to hire some men for him, friends of his who needed jobs he said. In return he canceled some of my gambling debts."

"What about the murders of Wong and Anderson?"

A look of fright spread across Clarkson's face, and he shook his head.

"I think you're hiding things, and I think you're lying. I don't like liars." Bolan stepped closer and sighted on the older man's nose. "Here's the deal. You tell me everything you know, and I'll protect you from whatever D'Angelo throws your way. You hold back on me, and you won't live to regret it."

"That Mafia bastard will kill me if I say anything," Clarkson whispered, staring in fascination at the gun focused on his face.

"And I'll kill you if you don't. At least if you play it my way you have a chance of staying alive. Refuse again, and you won't have another opportunity."

Bolan stared over the pistol barrel at the terrified man. He was betting that Clarkson, rotten gambler that he was, would fall for the bluff. The warrior wouldn't execute him in cold blood, but Clarkson had no way of knowing that.

The industrialist looked into the hooded eyes watching him over the barrel of the silenced gun, and thought he read his death in Bolan's cold stare.

"All right. You win." Clarkson's shoulders slumped in defeat.

He spent the next half hour spilling his guts, prompted by Bolan's incisive questioning. An ominous picture of betrayal emerged.

Clarkson had been lured into D'Angelo's debt several years earlier when the Mafia man bought up various notes that Clarkson owed to other gamblers. At that time his company had been doing poorly and had missed several major Defense Department contracts.

The entrepreneur could barely afford his legitimate expenses, let alone large gambling losses.

At first the relationship had been mutually profitable, although highly illegal. D'Angelo had a group of contacts who provided him with information on Defense Department requirements, which he passed along to Clarkson. This data was extremely useful when responding to government Requests for Proposals, a costly and time-consuming business. Knowing what the government expected made it easier for Clarkson to submit a strong proposal. Again, D'Angelo proved his value when it came time to submit a Best and Final Offer, which determined the pricing of the development projects.

Apparently D'Angelo belonged to some consortium of contractors that shared information, although he never revealed the details to Clarkson. All the mobster had required was that the entrepreneur provide him with the technical specifications of the products he developed, as well as share any research data that the government passed to Clarkson Industries to assist in engineering the components.

Fueled by the shady inside knowledge the Mafia provided, Clarkson Industries had grown tenfold.

However, once Clarkson had been hooked and become dependent on their assistance, the Mafia had asked other favors. Trivial at first, D'Angelo's demands had grown insatiably. Clarkson had effectively lost control of his company to the mobster, buying his supplies where the don specified, hiring men recommended by him and firing others he didn't like.

Clarkson Industries had become a Mafia stronghold, a front for the crime syndicate. The government would never knowingly buy from a Mob-controlled corporation, but Clarkson Industries had provided a respectable front. Through Clarkson, and probably others, D'Angelo had a window into critical areas of the American defense industry.

Bolan was particularly interested in the ring of men who provided the secret electronics data that was key to the whole underground operation. Whoever they were, they must be either experts in their field, or highly placed in the government, or both.

However, D'Angelo had been careful to conceal the details of how he acquired the information. When Clarkson received any data, D'Angelo had been scrupulous about removing all traces that might identify the source of the intelligence. For now the covert intel network was just another mysterious dead end.

"These men you hired, what were they like?" Bolan asked, returning to an earlier point in the discussion.

The other man spread his hands in a gesture of openness. Now that he had decided to cooperate, he was trying to convince Bolan that he was holding nothing back. The gun in Bolan's fist provided ample motivation.

"They were pretty ordinary," Clarkson said, "mostly in the engineering and quality-control departments. No one outstanding that I can recall, but competent enough."

Bolan grunted. It seemed crystal clear to the warrior that Clarkson didn't see what was going on. "I'll need their names and files tomorrow."

Clarkson looked apprehensive once again. "I don't know if I can do that. I'm getting a new assistant, or should I say spy, from D'Angelo in the morning."

"Then I'll go now and get the information myself. Give me your keys."

A few minutes later Bolan was traveling toward the plant after a brief stop to change into his colonel's uniform.

His unexpected arrival surprised the gate guard. Bolan stayed in character and announced that he was on a night inspection. He proceeded to make life miserable for the unfortunate man before storming off to tour the interior of the plant.

A few minutes later, alone in the personnel section, he extracted and photographed the relevant files with the aid of a minicamera. The data he had collected tonight would make some people jump through the roof back in Washington.

He doubted that the Pentagon would be thrilled to hear that the Mafia had plugged into a network specializing in trading defense secrets for mutual profit. Everyone had heard horror stories of the military paying four hundred dollars for an ordinary hammer. Most people would believe that the Mafia had infiltrated the military-industrial complex simply because there was so much money to be made.

However, Bolan suspected darker forces were at work, behind the ordinary profit motive.

What reason could there possibly be to infiltrate trained engineers into a high-tech installation? Industrial espionage unknown even to Clarkson but intended for use in some of D'Angelo's legitimate enterprises? It remained a possibility, but didn't smack of Mafia methods.

Something far more sinister lay beneath the surface of the investigation. Bolan had a feeling that even D'Angelo was only a part of the puzzle. Maybe someone else was pulling his strings, much as the crime boss had done with Clarkson.

He would have to keep digging, but with an eye on his back. Clarkson had confirmed that D'Angelo intended to eliminate him. The mafioso had tried once and failed because he had played it too subtly, attempting to make Bolan's demise look like an accident.

Next time D'Angelo wouldn't make the same mistake.

TONY D'ANGELO DIDN'T FEEL especially happy. He'd just spoken with a panicky Clarkson. The company chairman had revealed that Pollock wasn't an investigator, as he had claimed. Spy, federal agent, commando or whatever, Pollock knew all about their association and had demanded further information.

Of course, Clarkson said, he hadn't breathed a word.

D'Angelo debated whether to order Clarkson killed immediately. He knew the man well enough from their regular poker games to be able to recognize exactly when he was bluffing. D'Angelo was almost certain that Clarkson had spilled every bit of fact and rumor in his possession.

The don pondered the implications and considered whether he *would* be better off with Clarkson dead. The information that the industrialist might reveal would be damaging if the matter ever came to trial. But he decided to let Clarkson live for a while. He was reluctant to kill the golden goose before he had extracted every last egg.

Besides, a couple of his plans were about to hatch.

By tonight, whatever Pollock had learned should be absolutely irrelevant.

BOLAN PICKED UP the tail as soon as he left Clarkson Industries the next day. A man in a blue pin-striped business suit folded his paper and rose from a bus stop bench. He sauntered along after the warrior with the air of a man taking a casual lunch-hour stroll.

Bolan had spent a quiet morning observing the eight men Clarkson had identified as placed in the company by D'Angelo. From all appearances they were ordinary men doing average jobs. However, their positions allowed them access to every important component that the corporation manufactured. Any special projects that Clarkson might undertake would be reported back to D'Angelo in full detail.

The Executioner planned to question the men about their duties for D'Angelo, and he'd lean on them after business hours, much as he had with Clarkson.

The big man paused outside the door of a restaurant to inspect the posted menu. His shadow mirrored his move.

He stopped by a hot dog cart for a frank, while watching his tail from behind a pair of mirrored aviator shades. Abruptly Bolan dashed across the street, making for a short tunnel that led under a railway embankment into a deserted ravine park on the far side.

His shadow followed a moment later.

Across the street, a city cleaner abandoned his garbage cart and hurried toward the tunnel, while a young man in blue jeans and black jacket strolled away from his seat on a low wall, ghetto blaster in hand.

Bolan noted the movements. He reached the tunnel first and trotted in as his opponents converged.

The warrior had almost reached the end of the tunnel when the first assailant into the passageway opened fire. The silenced pistol coughed softly, the sound obliterated by the roar of traffic. The bullet gouged chips from the concrete wall.

Bolan didn't stop to return fire. Average citizens walked the streets at the other end of the tunnel. He had no intention of risking their lives with a stray bullet.

As the Executioner emerged and ducked behind a shady oak, he unleathered his Beretta 93-R and waited.

In moments a head popped briefly out of the tunnel, scanning for his location. Bolan held his weapon steady, concentrating on the end of the tunnel.

The edge of a radio poked out, trying to draw his fire, but Bolan restrained the impulse to squeeze the finely balanced trigger.

The man in the maintenance uniform came through in a shallow dive, while the guy in the leather jacket laid down random covering fire.

The Executioner focused on the maintenance man rolling for cover and loosed a 3-round burst. The gunman clutched his shattered chest before he crumpled to the ground in a heap. He wouldn't move again until an ambulance came for the body.

Bolan faded back among the trees. He intended to change position after every shot, since even the soft sigh of the Beretta could be pinpointed by a wary professional.

The man in the tunnel continued to spit random shots in the warrior's general direction, although he didn't have a prayer of inflicting any damage on his target.

The Executioner suspected that the guy was merely providing a distraction. His blue-suited companion was probably engaged at the moment in a flanking sweep.

Bolan scanned the little ravine, anticipating the moves the enemy might make. There were two alternate ways in for a determined aggressor. One was a shallow culvert that delved under the railway embankment, while the other crossed the embankment through a hole torn in the fence beside the tracks.

Bolan, like any trained soldier, knew the value of seizing the high ground. The warrior would have bet that his opposition would be coming over the top any time now. He ignored the sniping of the man in the tunnel, except for an occasional shot to make him believe that his target had fallen into the trap.

Two minutes later Bolan's patience was rewarded as a head poked cautiously around the edge of a railway shed above him. Blue suit ducked back and forth twice, trying to spot Bolan, before he finally decided to make a dash for the gap in the fence.

The Executioner, an expert marksman, let his target get fully in sight before he cut him down with a single shot. Blue suit skidded off his feet and crashed to the ground, tangling in the barbs of the torn fence.

Bolan had had enough, deciding to put an end to the miniwar before the lone remaining gunman figured out that he had better flee for his life.

The warrior flitted silently from tree to tree, conscious that his Air Force uniform made him more visible among the greenery than he would have liked. He planned a flanking move of his own, angling through the scattered trees to a point where he enjoyed a free shot at the gunner in the tunnel.

He had to move quickly before his quarry bolted. He sank behind the large elm that had been his destination and waited, his Beretta seeking the target.

A moment later the gunfight was over, as the young man poked his head toward the edge of the tunnel and the Executioner blew him away in a red splash.

Bolan contemplated the dead men as he rushed along a narrow path leading to an exit at the far end of the park. D'Angelo, or whoever was behind the second attempt, was intent on supporting a losing cause. But because the Executioner had hurt the enemy twice now, removing the opposition with almost contemptuous ease, the mobster would be enraged. Bolan had learned that the egos that lurked behind the twisted minds of the crime bosses couldn't stomach being bested.

D'Angelo had failed to bring him down, but Bolan knew beyond a doubt that he hadn't given up yet.

The mafioso remained his primary target for the moment, but he'd have to resist the compelling temptation to eliminate the don's criminal horde until he had unearthed the deeper connection that lay behind the infiltration of Clarkson Industries.

5

Tony D'Angelo regarded Mrs. Clarkson appreciatively. The woman had the figure of a model and no doubt had a lovely smile as well, when she chose to use it.

Right now she looked angry enough to spit in his face.

"What do you want with me? The police will lock you up for fifty years after I'm through with you," she shouted angrily when one of D'Angelo's men removed the gag from her mouth. Eight years ago she had been Clarkson's secretary. The spunk that had won him away from his former wife hadn't faded with time.

"Be quiet, Mrs. Clarkson," D'Angelo said softly, opening and closing a switchblade. "Otherwise I'll cut out your tongue."

The woman snapped her mouth shut.

D'Angelo slammed the knife deep into a pad of paper and then picked up the telephone and dialed a number. "Tom, it's Tony. I'm calling to tell you about a visitor who's just come to stay with me for a while. I picked her up at the airport. Would you like to say hello to your wife?"

"You have Janet? That's impossible. My driver picked her up an hour ago." Clarkson sounded just a bit too definite.

"Correction. *My* driver picked her up an hour ago."

After a long pause, Clarkson demanded to speak to her. The edge in his tone revealed his fear that the mafioso was telling the truth.

D'Angelo held out the receiver to Mrs. Clarkson. "Here, honey, hubby wants a word with you."

Janet Clarkson trembled as she took the phone and held it to her ear. "T-Tom."

"Janet?"

She began to sob. "Tom, please get me out of here. I don't understand what's—"

"That's enough."

D'Angelo grabbed back the phone to Janet's screams while Clarkson yelled, "Hold on! Everything is going to be fine. I promise."

"How sweet the words of love," the mobster interjected. "She can't hear you, Tom, but I'll be sure to pass along your assurances. She's a lovely creature, you know. I must admit that I could really enjoy being with a woman like her. You're a lucky man."

"Why, you bastard. I swear I'll kill you if you so much as lay a finger on her."

The Mafia boss listened for a moment, looking faintly amused. "I wouldn't make any boasts you can't carry out. It could damage your wife's health."

The entrepreneur lapsed into silence.

"That's better. Don't worry, I won't touch the merchandise, as long as you keep your mouth shut."

"But I told you I haven't said anything, and I meant it." Something in Clarkson's tone told D'Angelo a very different story.

"You told me a lot of things, Tom. I'm just making sure that you keep your promise to your pretty young wife here. Everything will be fine if you just make certain to remember a few small details. First, you have no business dealings with me whatsoever, no matter what evidence Pollock claims to have. We're just good friends. Deny everything else. And second, don't even think of telling the authorities some wild kidnapping tale, because I'll know if you do. It would be such a pity to have to say goodbye to Janet." D'Angelo let the threat hang in the air for a moment before he quietly replaced the receiver.

"Take her somewhere she won't be disturbed," D'Angelo said to one of his men. "By the way," he added as the captive reluctantly moved toward the door, propelled by two strong men. "if she gives you any trouble, you have my permission to carve up that pretty face a little."

When Mrs. Clarkson left, a look of pure terror had replaced her previous expression of angry contempt.

D'Angelo turned to his paperwork, convinced that spunky Janet Clarkson would be no trouble at all.

BOLAN FROWNED as he replaced the receiver. Brognola had drawn a blank on the names of the men appointed to positions of trust at Clarkson Industries on Tony D'Angelo's recommendation. Every one appeared to be as innocent as a baby.

What was the likelihood that half a dozen average men wouldn't have at least one blemish on their records? There wasn't even an unpaid parking ticket in the lot. Their seeming innocence heightened his suspicions. In any case, men referred by D'Angelo were bound to be dirty. There was no way that they were merely in need of jobs.

The police, via Brognola, had provided a little more information on the killers who had attacked Bolan in the park. Two remained unidentified, adding to the growing backlog in the morgue courtesy of the Executioner. The third had been tagged as imported muscle, a hit man who usually operated in the Midwest.

The don's minions would have to do a lot if they intended to take out the Executioner.

In the meantime, the warrior decided that it was time to kick ass among the hirelings that D'Angelo had dumped on Clarkson. Maybe one of them would supply a missing piece of the puzzle.

He selected one Jimmy Beam for his first visit, on the grounds that he was the youngest and therefore possibly the easiest to break. Jimmy worked in the research and development section, improving missile guidance technologies.

The technician lived in a high-rise condominium protected by a standard security lock on the doors inside the parking garage. The feeble protection held up the big man for about two seconds before he broke in. A minute later he had jimmied the apartment door.

The warrior rapped the sleeping man sharply on the head with the butt of his gun. When he was certain Beam was unconscious, he pulled a piece of cord and some heavy tape from a pocket of his blacksuit and trussed the man into immobility.

Bolan then bundled Beam into a large sack and trundled him into the garage without incident. A few minutes' drive brought Bolan and his passenger to a rickety bridge closed for repairs over a narrow canal. In the faint moonlight the dark water below looked like slowly moving oil.

The calm night was on the chilly side although Bolan was warm enough in his blacksuit. Beam would be a little cool in his pajamas, but that should provide another incentive for cooperation. Bolan didn't want the man comfortable, although the headache from the rap with the Beretta would ensure he suffered for a few hours.

He tied Beam firmly by the ankles with a stout nylon rope, then held a small bottle of smelling salts under the stunned man's nose to bring him around. For the occasion the warrior had concealed his face under a black mask to prevent the technician from recognizing him.

Beam's eyes snapped open. He looked around in panic and bewilderment. Muffled grunts escaped from behind the strip of wide adhesive tape that had been placed over his mouth. The young man thrashed about ineffectually.

"I want to know why D'Angelo got you into Clarkson Industries," Bolan demanded, ignoring Beam's frantic attempts to escape his bonds. "You tell me what I want to know, and you can go unharmed."

The technician had settled down and was watching his captor suspiciously, as though disbelieving.

"I'm going to remove the tape from your mouth," Bolan continued. "We're in the middle of nowhere, so there's no use screaming for help."

He bent over and ripped off the tape.

Beam grunted again but lay quietly.

"Talk," Bolan ordered.

The bound man shrugged. "There's nothing suspicious or illegal about my working at Clarkson. D'Angelo got me a job as a favor to a good friend of mine, his cousin. It's as simple as that."

"I don't believe you," the warrior said. An edge to Beam's voice made it perfectly clear that he was lying.

The technician shrugged again. "That's it, that's the whole story. If you don't believe me, that's your problem."

Bolan didn't bother to dispute the younger man's lack of information. He dragged Beam to the side of the bridge, where he took the end of the cord binding the man's hands and tied it firmly to the railing. The technician was slim and wiry, barely more than half Bolan's weight. Beam yelled at the top of his lungs, demanding that he be put down.

Bolan was unimpressed and proceeded to throw the screaming figure over the side of the bridge.

The nylon rope snapped taut on the iron rail and brought Beam to an abrupt halt just under the edge of the bridge. Swinging back and forth like a pendulum, his head down toward the black water below, the young man yelled in terror.

"I'm going to ask those questions one more time," Bolan called, catching Beam's attention. "If I believe you, I'll haul you up. Otherwise I let go of the rope, and someone will find your body in a few days. You understand?"

"Pull me up, for God's sake," Beam pleaded.

"Why did D'Angelo get you a job at Clarkson?"

"He wanted me to make sure that certain components passed acceptance tests, even if I had to falsify them." Beam had lost all pretense at defiance, but Bolan still thought he was holding back.

"What kinds of components?"

"Military electronics for missiles and jet fighters mostly."

"So you were sending electronics to the Air Force knowing they wouldn't work?" Bolan wondered still what the point of faking these tests would be. What could the Mafia possibly gain?

"Not every test," the technician protested, anxious to remove some of the tinge of guilt. "Only some tests under very special conditions."

"But you faked the tests for those?"

"Well, yes," Beam admitted reluctantly. "Now will you pull me up?"

"Not so fast. Explain a little more."

"Sometimes I could get something to work just by running the same test over and over until I got lucky. Then I'd sign it off and get my boss, who was in on the scam, to verify the results. Other times I'd just make up some numbers if I couldn't get it to go right. If that didn't work, I'd change the test conditions until it did."

"So you were faking it?" Bolan prodded.

"Whenever D'Angelo said so, yes."

Bolan digested the serious implications of Beam's story. Any weapon that had a Clarkson component could fail.

"What did you give to D'Angelo?"

The technician paused for a moment while he tried to think of a plausible lie.

Bolan wasn't biting. He let five feet of rope slip through his gloved hands, dropping Beam with a sharp jerk.

"All right," the man shrieked. "I gave him the test results."

"And?"

"I gave him the schematics and a copy of the components as well. Are you satisfied? D'Angelo is going to cut out my liver if he finds out what I've told you."

The Executioner hauled away on the rope. He wouldn't have dropped Beam to his death, but the young man hadn't cared to test Bolan's ethics with his life literally swinging in the balance.

A moment later he pulled Beam over the side of the bridge and replaced the tape gag. He guessed that he had squeezed everything of use from his captive. Beam didn't seem to have the spunk to lie convincingly under stress.

Bolan dropped off Beam at the parking garage, still bound and gagged. Someone would find him by morning, and it wouldn't do the unscrupulous technician any harm to suffer just a little more for his underhanded conduct.

As he dumped Beam heavily by the elevator door, Bolan told him to remain on the job as usual. Otherwise more questions might have to be asked, but not as gently.

Bolan wanted to leave D'Angelo guessing about how much he had found out from Beam.

The Executioner felt reasonably satisfied with his night's work. He had determined that D'Angelo was exploiting the research at Clarkson Industries and at the same time concealing defects in the components supplied to the military.

However, he could hardly be happy with the information he had gleaned. Lives depended on the correct functioning of the components of military equipment and weapons. Good men had died only days earlier in the crash of the experimental helicopter. There was no way of knowing how many more lives might be lost if this subversion continued. As a former soldier, he had a keen appreciation of the frustration of finding that a weapon suddenly won't work, usually at the moment when you need it most.

Possibly any flaws concealed by the functional testing at the manufacturer would be exposed during later testing. On the other hand, such a bug might skip through all subsequent checks until a weapon arrived in the hands of an American soldier, as deadly as a sleeping snake.

The Department of Defense spent about four billion dollars a year operating its far-flung networks of testing facilities, and yet problems still surfaced in combat, often sending men to their graves.

During the Falklands war the British destroyer *Sheffield* had been sunk by an Argentine missile because someone forgot to program the electronic intercept system to recognize the Exocet missile as a threat. Because the Exocet was manufactured by the French, an ally, someone had assumed that it wouldn't be employed against the British.

More recently, thirty-seven seamen had died aboard the U.S.S. *Stark* when two Iraqi jets had fired Exocet missiles launched at nearly the speed of sound from ten miles away. Fortunately one didn't explode.

The ship's advanced SLQ-32 V-2 electronic warfare system failed to detect the missile launch, for reasons unknown. Crewmen claimed that the missile had not even shown up on their monitors. Nor had the missile shown up on the ship's SPS-49 air search radar or SPS-55 surface search radar, supposedly among the most advanced systems in the world.

The automated Phalanx gun represented the *Stark*'s last-ditch defense. Equipped with its own radar, the gun was rated as able to spew an almost solid stream of lead, fifty rounds of 20 mm bullets every second. The Phalanx didn't respond to the missile threat, and when the ship was struck, not a single shot had been fired in self-defense.

Bolan remembered a case that had come to light several years ago, involving the development of brakes for a jet fighter. Pressure to produce had been so intense that officials of the manufacturer had faked test data, showing that the brakes met specifications, rather than admit they couldn't meet the deadline for delivery. A test pilot had almost been killed when the brakes failed during the first live test.

Within the past few years, the Department of Defense had scrapped several projects. Nearly two billion dollars had been wasted in development costs for systems that couldn't even meet minimal requirements.

Bolan reported the information Beam had come up with by telephone to Hal Brognola. Clearly major national security issues had surfaced involving possibly critical weapons systems. Sooner or later a full investigation would have to be quietly launched to determine to what extent the U.S. armed forces had already been compromised.

Unfortunately for defense programs, Clarkson Industries had access to parts of the so-called "black" programs. These were weapons systems under development that were considered so secret that even the kind of system being constructed was highly classified.

The Communists badly outgunned the West in terms of fighters, tanks, artillery and most other heavy weapons. The U.S. and its allies relied on a technological edge to maintain the balance of power.

It wasn't much of an advantage to have advanced weapons if none of them would function in combat.

Brognola at first proposed monitoring all of the men identified as linked with D'Angelo, as well as the Mafia don himself, until more information could be gathered.

Bolan argued that that would be a losing play. If D'Angelo learned that he was under suspicion, he could probably arrange for every scrap of evidence to disappear. D'Angelo's operatives at Clarkson would become targets for elimination as the mob leader tried to erase any trail leading back to him.

Bolan and Brognola would then lose any opportunity to dig beneath the surface of the case and learn why the Mafia had become involved in industrial espionage.

What puzzled the warrior was why D'Angelo had gone to the trouble to ensure that defective parts were passed to the military. Where did the advantage to D'Angelo lie?

Even now, the mobster might decide to cut the operation loose. It all depended on his motivation and whether the criminal mastermind felt he could keep the situation under control.

Bolan signed off after convincing Brognola that their only viable option remained fast, covert and decisive action. A dozen FBI agents sniffing around D'Angelo would simply drive him to ground.

The big man finally settled down for some shut-eye. Fifty different ways to rattle D'Angelo's cage ran through his brain, making sleep elusive.

6

"What is it, Jimmy, that's so important you couldn't tell me over the phone?" D'Angelo asked patiently. He tied the folds of his dressing gown a little more tightly and yawned widely. To men who didn't know him very well, the little don could seem benign and even a little slow-witted, an easy man to underestimate.

D'Angelo occasionally found such a manner a useful tactic when he wished to place someone at ease. "Bring some coffee for me and Jimmy," he said to no one in particular. The coffee appeared almost magically.

"Some nut case grabbed me in the middle of the night," Beam said carefully over his steaming mug, an anxious tremor in his voice. "He held me upside down over a bridge and tried to make me talk."

"I don't suppose you told him anything?" D'Angelo asked mockingly.

Jimmy missed the undertone. "No, of course not. He knew I worked for you and he threatened me, but I didn't say anything. I came here to warn you."

"What did this man look like?" D'Angelo demanded. He was sure Beam had come because he was frightened of what the Mafia leader might do if he found out about the nighttime visitor from another source.

"He was dressed all in black, and even had a mask. A big guy, and strong."

D'Angelo stared at Beam, turning things over in his mind. From the brief description, he concluded that Beam's assailant was the same man who had been plaguing him for the past few days.

The don sighed. He had hoped to salvage his relationship with Clarkson Industries, but matters had reached crisis proportions. The Mafia connection was so deeply exposed that there appeared little likelihood that the U.S. government would buy so much as a nail from Clarkson in future.

D'Angelo had run out of options.

Once Clarkson and his plant had represented an opportunity for millions in windfall profits through the information his sources in the company provided. Now the company represented a liability, a tenuous link that just might tie the don to a jail sentence. When he was a young man, he had spent a brief time in prison, kicking and clawing for survival. He had no intention of repeating the experience.

He signed to the muscle men in the room, and they dragged Beam out to a holding area behind the estate. Beam's protests faded as he vanished out of sight.

"Carlo," D'Angelo said, beckoning to an under-boss, "get the rest of the men up. It's going to be a busy morning. Then I want you to question Beam and find out what really happened."

"And then?"

D'Angelo silently drew his thumb across his throat.

THE INSISTENT RINGING of the telephone jerked Bolan wide awake. He glanced at the clock beside the bed—two and a half hours had elapsed since he'd spoken with Brognola.

When he raised the receiver to his ear, he heard the agitated voice of Hal Brognola. "Striker, we've got a problem."

"What is it?"

"I just heard that Jimmy Beam was found in a Dumpster half an hour ago with two small-caliber bullets in his head, execution style. From what I've heard, a witness saw him shortly after you dropped him off. Beam then drove away from the apartment building in a big hurry."

Bolan grunted, hardly surprised at the news. One man in the city had a powerful motive for Beam's death. The warrior was sure that the timing of the technician's murder, just hours after their meeting, was more than simple coincidence.

In fear, Beam had probably called D'Angelo to report the encounter, and the don had rewarded the man with a brace of slugs in the head, silencing his wagging tongue forever.

"I suppose this means that the other men are in danger as well," Bolan suggested. D'Angelo would probably roll up his little network in the most decisive way imaginable: dead men couldn't testify in court against him.

"My thought exactly," Brognola agreed. "I've only got limited resources in the area, and I've dispatched them to cover all but one of the men in danger. Can you take the last man?"

Bolan agreed immediately. Neither he nor the man from Justice wanted the local police involved at this stage. The national security aspect to the case might mean endless repercussions as well as a certain curtailment of Bolan's autonomy.

He could hardly deal with D'Angelo as he intended with the police looking over his shoulder. Bolan and the police agreed on the necessity for stopping crime and punishing the criminals, but they parted company on how best to accomplish the task.

Bolan wasn't a civil libertarian, he was a pragmatist. He had little regard for the rights of savage killers: his sympathies lay entirely with the unfortunate victims of crime.

Every killer he removed from circulation meant one less cannibal devouring the heartland of America. Too many still preyed on the hundreds of thousands of people reduced to hiding behind locked doors because of crime running rampant in every corner of American cities.

Bolan changed quickly and dropped into the hotel lobby to get a new rental car. He knew D'Angelo would love to send flowers to his funeral. Self-preservation dictated that the warrior switch rentals every day and keep a low profile.

When the car arrived he checked it over rapidly but thoroughly, just in case D'Angelo's men had tagged him and rigged the vehicle with an explosive surprise.

He steered through Saturday morning midtown traffic with as much haste as he could muster until he reached the quiet residential street where Henry Jaworski, an engineer in the testing department, lived with his wife and young child. Three-story town houses lined the road amid spreading chestnut trees. Mothers played with children on well-tended lawns, and senior citizens walked their dogs.

The Executioner wasn't reassured by the tranquil surroundings. Before he left his hotel he had called Jaworski's home to warn the family of impending trouble—no one had answered in twenty rings.

It was possible that the family had simply taken a walk for ice cream or were performing the dozens of errands that occupied the weekends of most American families. But Bolan suspected a more sinister explanation for Jaworski's absence. The warrior was convinced that most of D'Angelo's connections had already been eliminated. If Jaworski had survived this long, he was a lucky man.

He scanned the vicinity of Jaworski's home as he slowed to find a parking space. Two men sat reading newspapers in a dark Cadillac halted almost directly across from the engineer's house. It looked as though he had arrived in time to intercept Jaworski. Enforcers would hardly be watching the engineer's home if they had made the hit already.

Bolan angled into a slot two spaces behind the Cadillac. Eyes in the big car followed his movements with interest as he crossed the street and walked up the steps to Jaworski's house.

He looked briefly over his shoulder and observed one of the pair speaking into a small walkie-talkie. That confirmed his expectation that some of D'Angelo's men were waiting inside for Jaworski to return.

Bolan had debated whether to try skirting around the back or to make a direct approach. If he came from the rear and someone was posted to keep the back door under surveillance, he stood a good chance of being gunned down before he could get inside.

On the other hand, the hit men sent after the engineer probably wouldn't have much of a description, just an address and orders to kill. Bolan figured that he could march right up to the front door unmolested, with the gunners thinking that he was walking into a firing squad.

The men inside planned to ambush whoever walked through the door. Bolan bet that he could reverse the surprise on the waiting killers.

He spent a moment jimmying the lock until the bolt slid back with a satisfying thunk. He drew the Beretta from under his jacket and slipped it into his pocket, carefully using his body to screen his actions from the men in the car. Through the door he could hear the angry wail of a child.

Bolan barged through shouting, "Honey, I'm home," to add a little realism to his entrance and found himself inside a small foyer. He closed the street door and shoved open the inner door.

Two men stood ten feet inside the entryway, weapons leveled on his stomach. "Hands up," one commanded with a grin.

Bolan fired through his pocket and dived for the floor in one motion.

A gasp of pain and astonishment sounded as one killer toppled with a 9 mm slug chewing his guts. His companion fired high in his surprise, splintering the pressboard door behind Bolan.

The Executioner fired as he rolled over the thin beige carpet, and the second hit man collapsed, sporting a third eye in the middle of his forehead.

Bolan's first target struggled to raise his gun for a final shot before his life ebbed away.

The warrior triggered one more round from the Beretta and the .22-caliber execution weapon slipped from the enforcer's limp grasp.

Rising slowly, Bolan waved his pistol in quest for more targets. Other than the steady crying of the child in an upstairs room, the house was silent.

He exited the narrow hall, stepping over the two inert bodies.

He found Mrs. Jaworski facedown on the living room rug, bound and gagged. Blood stained her short brown hair from two bullet wounds to the head. He checked for vital signs but wasn't surprised to feel no pulse.

A walkie-talkie on a chair emitted a short burst of static and then a man announced that another guy was moving toward the house.

Bolan threw a patterned quilt from the sofa over the dead woman. As he spread it, the handle of the front door rattled.

"Honey, I'm home," a man called from the hall, echoing Bolan's entrance.

"What the hell—" the man said almost immediately as Jaworski saw the dead hit men sprawled on the floor.

Bolan stepped into the hall, his gun in hand. He wanted to maintain control of the situation and felt it best to intimidate Jaworski from the start with his weapon. Jaworski stood there with a bag of golf clubs on his back and a shocked expression on his face.

"Get in here," Bolan ordered, gesturing with the gun.

Jaworski obeyed silently. "I know you," the engineer said as he edged by, carefully keeping his hands in sight. "You're the Air Force guy who's been nosing around. What the hell's going on?"

"I've learned all about your arrangement with D'Angelo," Bolan said, seeing the shock register on Jaworski's features. "Things have gone sour, and he's put out a contract on all his men at Clarkson. Those are the killers sent for you," he said, pointing at the corpses in the hall. "I'm here to protect you and take you somewhere where you'll be safe."

A look of horror crossed Jaworski's face. "How can I trust you?" he said dubiously.

"If I had wanted to kill you, you'd be dead now," Bolan answered simply.

The engineer grunted in acknowledgment. "All right, what do I do?"

"Get your child from upstairs and follow my directions exactly. Go on." Bolan moved to the window and peered cautiously through the curtains. The men in the car hadn't moved.

Less than a minute later, Jaworski clumped down the stairs carrying a small child in his arms. The boy still yelled at the top of his voice. "Where's Marg, my wife?'' he asked nervously. "I haven't seen her yet. Will she meet us wherever we're going?"

"She's dead," Bolan said bluntly. "They killed her before I got here." He refrained from pointing out that it was Jaworski's involvement with organized crime that had resulted in her murder.

The engineer looked stunned at first and then tears welled in his eyes.

Bolan didn't have much patience, considering the circumstances. "Snap out of it," he said, deliberately harsh. "Do you want to get your son killed, too?"

Jaworski gulped a few times and regained some of his composure.

"That's better. Now I'm going out to get my car. When I pull up in front, get in the back seat and keep your head down. Move fast when the coast is clear. There are at least two other killers waiting for you."

Bolan studied Jaworski's face to see if he was absorbing his instructions. He wouldn't have time to baby-sit the man when the shooting started. "Don't be a hero. There's nothing you can do. Understood?"

Jaworski nodded and Bolan headed off. He sped down the short flight of steps, figuring that the unexpected sight of someone other than their own men leaving the house would give the Mafia watchers something to think about for a precious moment.

The warrior would squeeze every ounce of advantage out of whatever seconds they granted him.

He made a dash for his car, opened the door and slid into the driver's seat in one easy motion. The car jumped to life with a twist of the ignition key, and he gunned it over to the opposite side of the street, directly in front of Jaworski's house.

The mafiosi had finally reacted to the unexpected development. The driver steered the Cadillac in a screeching curve, ending with the big car angled against the sidewalk blocking Bolan's getaway.

The Executioner wasn't planning to go anywhere without Jaworski and his child. He bolted from the car, drawing his massive Desert Eagle .44. Crouching behind a fender, he targeted on the other driver, who had gained a firing position behind the open door of the Cadillac.

The gunner let loose with an Uzi machine pistol, the slugs whining angrily over Bolan's head.

The Desert Eagle boomed once and the heavy slug carved through the Cadillac's window, crunching into the driver's chest amid a shower of glass chips. Bolan shifted targets before the first man hit the ground.

His second opponent had been a little slow off the mark. The enforcer opened fire with his own mini-Uzi as the Executioner swiveled in his direction. Bolan fired the semiautomatic pistol once, but that was all he needed to finish the gunfight. The Magnum slug impacted at the base of the mafioso's throat, putting an abrupt halt to the hail of lead.

Jaworski had wisely remained under cover during the battle. Now he ran from the house with the child bundled in his arms, and flung himself and the boy into the back of Bolan's sedan.

The warrior jumped into the vehicle and reversed it, thankful that the Uzi's slugs hadn't damaged anything vital. More Mafia soldiers might be in the vicinity, and he had no desire to try to outrun any pursuers in a wounded car.

He passed several frightened suburbanites, sensibly flat on the ground after the sudden burst of gunfire that had shattered the quiet morning.

A quick glance in the rearview mirror to check for signs of pursuit revealed a dark sedan turning in behind him, running a second car up on the curb in a blaze of horns in its haste.

Company was coming.

Bolan steered down an alley, trying first to evade the opposition—he had two civilians to protect.

He stepped on the gas, barely skimming by clustered garbage cans and precarious heaps of piled boxes. Before he cleared the last obstacle, the car following him turned into the lane right on his tail.

The big man didn't like his options. He could either try to lose the other car in traffic, which meant that he might be involved in a showdown in the middle of a crowded street, or keep to the back roads of a town he didn't know very well and possibly find himself in a dead end.

Bolan decided to keep to the main thoroughfares and try to outrun the opposition.

He gunned the rental as he turned onto a main route, picking up speed as he accelerated, heedless of any traffic cops that might put in an appearance. He wove among the slower cars, earning the wrath of several white-knuckled motorists.

The mafioso at the wheel of the pursuit vehicle was more than competent and as reckless as Bolan. The powerful luxury car following the warrior—with a little more juice than Bolan's own midrange sedan—actually gained a bit in the chase, trailing Bolan's car by about two hundred yards. He had hit a succession of green lights, a rare event on a city street, and unwelcome on this occasion.

Just ahead, the lights switched to amber and Bolan put the pedal to the metal to squeeze every ounce of speed from the laboring engine. He popped through the intersection just after the traffic light changed to red.

The mobsters followed, oblivious to the glowing warning signal. The Cadillac entered the intersection at the same time as a fully loaded cement truck. The two vehicles met in a cataclysmic screech of tortured metal.

When Bolan looked in the rearview mirror as he slowed from the chase, all he could see was a bit of twisted metal poking from under the chassis of the oversize mixer.

Two more down.

D'Angelo had been nicked by the Executioner once again.

Soon it would be time to turn the trickle of blood into a torrent.

7

Bolan dropped off the shaken Jaworski and his son across town at a federal office. Some of Brognola's Justice Department confederates had returned from attempts to guard the renegade Clarkson Industries employees from D'Angelo's execution teams.

The warrior compared notes with the agents as they trickled in. None of the seven men Brognola's team had sought to protect had been saved. Two had been found shot to death in their homes, and five others had simply disappeared.

Three wives and two small children were also dead or missing, victims by simply being in the wrong place at the wrong time.

Ironically Clarkson himself had been rescued. His protectors had scooped him up before he left his secure compound for the danger of the streets. The industrialist's expensive bodyguards had earned their keep by holding off the Mafia hit men who lurked outside.

Clarkson had joined Jaworski in protective custody, where the pair would be singing loud to anyone who would listen. Bolan didn't bother to interview the industrialist; he was sure he had extracted everything of value already.

The big man refused to feel any sympathy toward Clarkson at the moment. He'd fallen hard, but he had also indirectly caused the deaths of several of his employees through his subservience to the Mafia don. On the run, with hired killers stalking his movements, Clarkson had paid a hefty price for his addiction to poker.

Treason charges might be added to the bill if it turned out that military secrets had fallen into the hands of interested foreign parties. Clarkson would have the opportunity to atone for his crimes with many years of hard time, unless he was lucky enough to be accepted into the federal witness protection program and live out his days in obscurity.

Bolan turned his mind from Clarkson and contemplated his next move. He had to put his Colonel Rance Pollock persona to rest. The colonel had outlived his usefulness.

Teams of shrewd investigators from the Justice Department would eventually go over every record with independent military evaluators to discover whatever Clarkson employees had concealed. It might take a long time to learn the extent of the damage Clarkson and D'Angelo had caused, but at least the spread of the disease had been halted.

But that was no longer the warrior's concern. He'd leave the paperwork for those more inclined to a life shackled to a desk. He decided that his first task should be a brief scouting mission to examine D'Angelo's hideaway. The don had shown himself to be decisive and ruthless, and it would be folly to launch a campaign without first examining the battlefield.

Brognola had already informed Bolan that nothing illegal could be traced to the secretive crime lord, certainly nothing that a few well-paid defense lawyers couldn't blow holes through.

D'Angelo's own men would never betray their oath of silence. Not only would it be a fatal mistake, it would also violate their own twisted sense of honor.

Brognola had no one on the inside who could supply a definite provable accusation. Such evidence, if it could be elicited from the tight-lipped criminals, would be a very long time in coming. Even the testimony of Clarkson and Jaworski might not be sufficient to ensure a conviction, at least one that would stick beyond a first appeal.

There was little chance that D'Angelo would ever serve a day in prison for the murders that he had ordered from his comfortable office. Unofficially, Brognola and half the state knew who stood behind the men who pulled the triggers.

But every man was entitled to the full protection of the law, even a monster like D'Angelo.

The Executioner didn't much care for the delicate balance of the scales of justice. In his mind the trial had already taken place. The verdict? Guilty.

All that remained was to carry out the death sentence.

As Bolan prepared to leave, one of the federal agents brought word that Clarkson urgently wanted to see him. The big man had no desire to hear the industrialist's sudden demands. However, he made his way back to the holding area on the off chance that Clarkson might provide a shred of useful information.

"You've got to help me," Clarkson began as soon as Bolan walked in.

"I don't have to do a damn thing, Clarkson," Bolan replied coldly. He raked his eyes over the man, who didn't look quite so proud and arrogant now that he was in protective custody, the forerunner of far worse to come.

"Sorry." Clarkson smiled ingratiatingly. "I mean you've got to help my wife. D'Angelo has her, if he hasn't killed her already."

Bolan raised an eyebrow.

"He planned to hold her hostage to guarantee that I wouldn't testify against him or admit to any kind of connection between us." Clarkson threw up his hands plaintively. "Now that I'm incarcerated, I don't know how long he'll leave her alone."

The Executioner considered the situation. D'Angelo might release the woman if only to prevent being slapped with a murder charge based on Clarkson's story. However, the don had shown himself to be merciless toward his enemies and might figure that vengeance demanded that Clarkson's wife die.

Bolan studied the industrialist carefully, trying to determine if his request were really a last twisted plot to lure him into an ambush. He realized that it was entirely possible that the man blamed Bolan rather than himself for the downfall of his empire.

The warrior decided that the guy was on the level. Clarkson quivered like a dog afraid of being beaten.

"Why not simply tell the Feds?" Bolan demanded. "Kidnaping is a serious federal offense."

Clarkson shrugged. "I think that if I told them I'd end up with a dead wife. D'Angelo has spies everywhere. Besides, I spoke with Jaworski. From what he told me, if any one person can rescue my wife, you're the man."

Bolan grunted, not pleased with the flattery. But he agreed to try to free Mrs. Clarkson. Her only crime was marrying a loser, and for that she didn't deserve to die.

After a brief discussion of her whereabouts, Bolan was left with two possibilities: she was being held at either the mansion or the chalet in the woods where the poker game had been held.

If Mrs. Clarkson wasn't at either place, he would never find her.

Bolan returned the damaged rented car with a rather weak story of a drive-by shooting to explain the bullet holes in the fender and smashed window. A fifty slipped to the clerk made the story a shade more believable, enough to prevent an immediate call to the police.

However, Bolan took his business across the street and picked out a sporty Corvette. If he needed speed again, he didn't want to be on the wrong end of a chase.

The day was young and bright, hardly ideal conditions for a rescue attempt. Storming the D'Angelo mansion was an act verging on suicidal, so he turned the long nose of the Corvette toward the outskirts of town. He could at least eliminate the country place as a possibility and make his assault on D'Angelo's stronghold in the evening if the chalet proved barren.

Bolan hid the sports car in a grove of trees well away from the hideout, then took the time to change into camouflage greens. He applied combat cosmetics to his face until he blended into the brush like a tree swaying in the breeze.

The Executioner carried an AR-15 as his lead weapon for this assault. The Beretta and Desert Eagle rode in their customary positions, and an assortment of spare clips, knives and other deadly gadgets were secured to the warrior's military webbing.

Ready, Bolan trotted off, prepared to face a small army if necessary. He slowly worked his way through the woods, treating the probe as though he knew with certainty that his quarry lay at the end of the heavily guarded road.

The ground was slightly familiar from his earlier visit, and halfway along the path to the chalet he noticed that D'Angelo had posted guards once again.

Two men sat quietly in the woods, holding machine pistols at the ready. Several large logs had been rolled across the road, forming a blockade. A vehicle wouldn't be able to pass without stopping for its driver to remove the barrier.

Any unwary trespassers could be cut down without warning by the hidden gunmen, who would be able to sweep the roadway with their weapons.

The warrior continued silently through the underbrush, his hopes buoyed by the presence of the manned outpost. It was hardly conclusive, but the evidence of armed hardmen made it far more likely that something worth guarding lay at the end of the trail. Birds chirped and wind rustled the leaves, drowning out the faint sounds of his passing.

A few minutes later, he edged into position among the ring of trees surrounding the chalet. Two innocuous sedans were parked in front of the house. One man sat on the steps smoking; a submachine gun lay cradled in his lap.

Bolan thought about the position from the point of view of the defenders, imagining how he would set about guarding an isolated building. The two cars could have held up to nine men and the woman. So far he'd seen only three of the defenders, although he would have bet that at least two remained indoors.

That left three or four men for roving patrols.

Bolan circled clockwise through the fringe of the woods, with the stealth of a forest hunter. A hard school where failure meant death had taught him field craft, and not a twig cracked under his feet as he edged from tree to tree.

His opponents, city-bred men more at home on concrete than grass, stood out like beacons in the woods. Bolan heard the first man wheezing and coughing before he saw him.

The warrior crept up behind the Mafia hardman. Something in the woods obviously didn't agree with him, and he had dropped his machine pistol to use both hands to blow his stuffed-up nose.

Bolan pulled out a small blackjack and hit the gunman solidly on the head while he was absorbed in his misery. The Mafia man toppled limply, and the warrior pounced on him. He applied tape to the stunned man's mouth and bound his hands to a tree with stout nylon.

The big man saw no need to kill unless he was confronted. If the opportunity presented itself, rendering an opponent immobile was sufficient for this mission.

One down. Bolan started out again, conscious that time ticked away slowly now that he had shown his hand. Sooner or later the guard would be missed and the alarm sounded.

The second guard proved even easier to deal with than the first. Bolan came upon him sleeping in a patch of sunlight with his back against a thick tree. He evidently hadn't considered the possibility of an intruder to be very serious.

So much the better for Bolan.

The gunman's eyes didn't even flutter when the warrior crashed the blackjack on his balding head. In scant minutes the mafioso was bound and gagged.

Bolan had worked his way behind the chalet. If the distance between guards was approximately equal, only one more man should remain in the ring of woods.

The warrior spotted him, a stocky nervous man who swung back and forth at the least sound. There would be no chance of creeping up on him unobserved. But it wasn't enough just to silence the guard. Bolan had to do it without allowing him to fire a shot and alert the gunmen inside with the hostage.

Any disturbance might result in Mrs. Clarkson's execution.

Bolan flitted from tree to tree until he stood only about twenty feet from the building, lost in the dappled shadows of the edge of the woods. He picked up a large stone and tossed it a few feet farther into the woods.

The guard's head swiveled at the noise. He hesitated a moment, then walked toward the spot where the rock had landed, his eyes darting in every direction.

Bolan stood still, blending into the fringe of brush as though he were a plant. As the Mafia man passed within reach, Bolan swung the blackjack. The club caught the guard on the side of the head as he turned toward the faint rustling, and he dropped before he could pull the trigger. Blood flowed from a ragged gash in his forehead.

Bolan had him trussed in a matter of moments.

He completed the circuit just in case one more guard remained. Satisfied that his back was protected, Bolan eased around to a point near one corner of the house.

Windows pierced each wall, but he expected that he could angle a run so that someone would have to be watching directly out the window to see him approach. And he had to keep out of sight of the single man sitting out front.

He broke cover and ran, crossing the fifty yards between the woods and the wall in seconds. The warrior paused, back to the wall, his finger on the trigger of the AR-15.

No alarm was raised.

He crept around to a back window and angled a small mirror to look through the heavy curtains, then drew the mirror down quickly. Someone stood just inside the curtains drinking from a mug. His quick glance had revealed that the room within was the kitchen.

Bolan dashed around to the side, passing one window, probably the kitchen again, and repeated his maneuver with the mirror at the next one. He studied the faint image carefully. Three men sat watching TV, absorbed by the raucous sounds of a game show.

None of the hardmen had weapons in hand, but no doubt they were within easy reach. The prisoner sat in a straight chair, her hands bound behind the rungs. As Bolan watched, a fourth man came from the kitchen.

The warrior considered how best to enter the house. The windows were fairly high above the ground—too much so to get through without difficulty. He decided that the only practical option was to use one of the doors.

With the kitchen clear, Bolan hurried around back. One of the steps creaked under his feet, but the sound of the television drowned out the squeak. The handle of the back door turned under his touch, and he eased it open and slid inside.

Bolan appeared in the doorway as though he'd materialized from thin air. He swung around the AR-15 to cover the mafiosi enraptured in the babble from the sixty-inch TV.

"Don't move," Bolan growled.

The gunmen turned and gaped at the combat-clad soldier. For a stunned half second there was complete silence, except for the game show host's penetrating voice. Then one man broke the spell and reached for a shoulder holster.

The assault rifle stuttered in Bolan's hands and the gunner fell backward, punched to the floor by the burst of slugs. Mrs. Clarkson screamed shrilly.

The other gunmen erupted into motion, diving for cover behind scattered pine furniture. Bolan tracked one with the AR-15, stitching a line of manglers up the killer's back as he fled.

The big man stepped forward and kicked over the woman's chair, toppling her with it. She would make less of a target behind the pedestal of the table.

The outdoor guardian fired through the front window, shooting a steady stream from his 9 mm Viking SMG. Bolan had already taken evasive action, diving and rolling under the edge of the table. The machine gun rounds cut the air harmlessly overhead.

The Executioner's return fire blazed back, more accurate—and deadly. The TV exploded into fiery shards of glass as he tracked the assault rifle across the back wall to the window. The gunman toppled back off the porch with a strangled cry.

Wood chips flew from the table as the last two gunners sought to bring Bolan down. One Mafia soldier fired a .38 pistol while the last clutched a stubby Ingram Model 10.

Bolan lay low momentarily until the machine gunner exhausted his magazine. In the lull, the Executioner poked the muzzle of his rifle around the table and snapped a burst at the pistol man, who had incautiously exposed himself to protect his companion as he reloaded.

Now the warrior was going one-on-one with the last gunner.

The mafioso poured out his full magazine in one long burst at Bolan's position, then he bolted for the shattered window, hoping to escape the Executioner's wrath.

Bolan wasn't letting anyone escape to warn the guards at the barrier or to ambush him as he made his getaway. He directed a burst at the fleeing man.

The gunman dropped clumsily through the window with an agonized yell.

The warrior paused momentarily to verify that danger had passed for the moment. The only sound was the bound woman's soft whimpering.

Before releasing her, he snapped a fresh magazine into the AR-15 in case further trouble awaited them on the path to freedom. Then he unleathered a large knife and cut Janet Clarkson's bonds.

She collapsed, sobbing, onto the floor. Bolan had to shake her not too gently to bring her back from the edge of hysteria.

"I'm here to rescue you," he shouted. "Snap out of it."

The attractive woman sniffed and wiped her nose on her sleeve, nodding meekly.

"Follow me," Bolan ordered.

He moved to the window and checked outside. There was no sign of reinforcements.

"Come on. We have to move quickly," he said, heading toward the front door. He paused briefly after swinging the door wide, then trotted down the steps, the AR-15 swinging over a wide arc in case of trouble.

Janet Clarkson followed slowly, averting her eyes from the two dead men heaped under the shattered window.

Bolan led the way into the woods, telling her to keep behind him but to stay close. He expected that they might attract some attention as they wandered back to the car.

A hundred yards farther on he halted as the sound of stealthy movements reached his ears. He motioned her to drop to the ground. Dressed in a pink top and white skirt, she was hard to miss against the brown-and-green background.

She stood frozen in panic, unable to move.

Bolan was afraid that she might scream. He hurried noiselessly back and dragged her to the forest floor, placing a hand over her mouth.

The Executioner remained motionless, keeping Janet Clarkson beneath him. He held the assault rifle steady with his right hand in case they were detected.

The two men from the barrier passed by twenty feet away, never suspecting that sudden death crouched nearby.

As soon as the sounds faded, Bolan hauled Mrs. Clarkson to her feet and propelled her at top speed through the woods, not pausing until they reached the Corvette at the edge of the forest.

The woman was gasping from the exertion, her clothes were torn from brambles and she limped after having lost a shoe.

However, she was alive.

After a few minutes' drive back to the safehouse, Bolan witnessed a tearful reunion between the husband and wife.

Shortly the woman was sent away to refresh herself, at which time Clarkson approached Bolan to offer his thanks. "What can I do to make up for this?" he asked, his eyes moist with emotion as he wrung Bolan's hand.

"Don't worry," Bolan responded, extracting his hand from the other man's grip. "I'll think of something."

8

Bolan left the federal hideout satisfied with his progress. He had dealt a damaging blow to D'Angelo and cleared the way for further operations.

Now the war would start in earnest.

He'd begin with a soft probe of the Mafia don's home turf, as he'd intended before Clarkson had diverted him.

Bolan drove fifteen miles west of the Loop to Oak Brook, a stately suburban retreat and home to many of Chicago's premier crime figures. The wealthy suburbs housed raketeers among the Frank Lloyd Wright homes, but the legitimate residents weren't too concerned.

One local police official had told Bolan that home values along the street where the crime lord lived rose twenty percent when D'Angelo moved in. His neighbors figured that no one would dare commit crimes in the don's neighborhood. Indeed, the subdivision enjoyed the safest streets in America.

Bolan intended to add a little excitement to the dreary lives of the suburbanites. When he had finished with D'Angelo, the neighbors might not be as eager to welcome the criminal class in the future.

D'Angelo's home appeared innocent enough, viewed in the distance nestled among a ring of mature evergreens. Three stories of red brick with a conical turret at one end, it squatted at the end of a long drive. A four-car garage flanked the house.

The driveway was protected by an iron gate, but the two hulking men lounging beyond the gate represented the real security. Bolan had no doubt that more men were on hand and would appear immediately if summoned.

A quick drive past the property provided almost no information. He'd have to go in on foot to gain any useful intelligence.

Bolan parked half a mile away, outside the area normally patrolled by the private police force of the wealthy community. The rich residents were a jumpy lot and would certainly report a suspicious car parked anywhere within their little enclave. He walked the streets casually, for all the world like a man out for a leisurely stroll.

A couple of houses away from D'Angelo's mansion, Bolan ducked down a right-of-way that led to a small ravine running behind the crime lord's property.

The big man scrambled down a steep slope to a path that followed alongside a narrow brook. He trudged along the tree-lined valley until he reckoned that he'd come abreast of D'Angelo's home.

He shinnied up a tall, leafy poplar tree until he could peer over the back wall. A large, kidney-shaped pool gleamed below him, reflecting the vibrant orange of the setting sun.

However, his interest lay in a different quarter.

He examined the complex with a pair of high-powered binoculars. The wall circling the estate was the first challenge to an intruder—a triple layer of barbed wire ran across the top of the eight-foot fence. A separate strand just inside probably represented a trip wire designed to sound the alarm in a guardhouse if the wall was breached.

Around the house, strategically placed cameras covered both the wall and the inner grounds, and banks of lights lined the eaves of the roof. Undoubtedly a security station somewhere in the complex maintained a constant watch over the monitors that scanned the grounds.

As Bolan watched, four men sauntered from the direction of the garage. The group split up, two moving to relieve the guards at the gate and the remaining pair walking toward the house. That meant there were at least eight guards available at any one time, and more likely a dozen.

Once D'Angelo received reports of the shoot-out at the country retreat, he might decide to ring his compound with men. The temptation would be to try to set an impenetrable guard that the Executioner wouldn't dare challenge.

Bolan lowered the binoculars. He'd learned everything he could from a passive reconnaissance. His next move would commit him to open warfare with the Mafia forces.

D'ANGELO FELT loathing as he picked up the ringing red telephone. "What do you want?" he demanded harshly.

"I understand that you have been acting very foolishly without consulting me first." The voice drifted into D'Angelo's ear, even and melodic, as always. The don could almost believe that a computer-generated voice spoke at the opposite end of the line.

At times D'Angelo wondered what temporary madness had led him into an unholy alliance with a partner whose strength he had come to fear.

Originally the mobster had thought that he was entering a partnership of equals. He had even expected to obtain the upper hand. In the past the don had succeeded in besting every man he had confronted; confidently he had expected to do the same forever.

Money had provided the bait and he had gladly taken it, expecting to be able to spit out the hook. The cash had flowed in waves, a small torrent from both legal and illegal sources that enriched his crime family beyond belief. Millions of dollars of taxpayers' money poured into his hands through his connections to the military armaments business.

His secret friends had provided the key to a hoard of gold. However, the Mafia chieftain sometimes thought their interference more trouble than the money they brought him was worth.

It wasn't that they controlled his daily operations or interfered with his normal business. However, a hint of violence, a constant threat, always hovered in the background.

"If you're talking about icing my men at Clarkson, I just took a sensible precaution." D'Angelo spoke without fear of detection. He knew that encryption devices at each end of the line scrambled the conversation so randomly that even the CIA couldn't decipher whatever secrets he spilled.

"I do not believe that those men were in any immediate danger," the man replied. "All you have served to accomplish is to eliminate an important source of information and jeopardize the entire operation."

"You let me worry about my business," D'Angelo snarled, provoked by the patronizing attitude of his partner.

"Do not anger me, D'Angelo," the caller returned. "Remember Caporetti." A long silence followed to give D'Angelo an opportunity to remember. "Your business *is* our business . . . at least as it relates to our agreement, which you have seriously threatened."

D'Angelo had only once challenged his associates. The next day Caporetti, his chief lieutenant, had been discovered in a small park near his home, his face obliterated by soft-nosed bullets fired at point-blank range.

"What was I supposed to do?" D'Angelo replied more softly, slightly chastened. "It was me the Feds would have been after next, not you."

"Let's just keep it that way, shall we? Remember, one word of our association and you are a dead man." The caller spoke matter-of-factly, as though he were absolutely certain that his threat would be executed.

The Mafia boss was equally certain that he stood no chance of carrying out a similar threat. He wasn't even entirely sure where his partner resided.

"Have you solved your Air Force problem?" the man queried.

"Not yet, but soon," D'Angelo replied.

"Then I shall do you a favor. I shall send a team to eliminate him. And next time, consult me before you do anything rash, or you will force me to send them after you." The caller paused ominously. "I don't think you would like to meet them. They are really not very nice people."

The line went dead.

D'Angelo cursed silently and dropped the receiver. He noticed that his palms were dripping with sweat.

BOLAN DESCENDED from his treetop observation post slowly, his mind occupied with alternative ways into the complex. When possible, he always avoided frontal assaults as dangerous and often unproductive. Surprise was desirable. He needed to come up with an appropriate ruse to distract the enemy.

The big man started back the way he had come, engrossed in thought. A bullet suddenly smacked into a nearby tree, and Bolan dived to the ground, keeping to a roll until he came to a halt at the base of a thick elm. His eyes scanned the surrounding trees for a sign of the ambusher.

D'Angelo obviously maintained a better guard than he'd anticipated. Someone had discovered his little foray into the woods and wasn't happy about it.

The tree line edging the ravine appeared silent and deserted. If someone held the high ground against him, Bolan was left with a difficult approach up the slopes. Against a determined opponent, that could prove a deadly challenge.

The Executioner drew his Beretta, the only weapon he had brought with him on what he had expected to be a soft probe. He rolled away from the shelter of the elm and scrambled for another large tree some ten feet away.

As soon as he broke cover, another shot blazed past his face. The angry crack of the rifle followed a moment later. Bolan recognized the pitch of the report as that of a high-velocity rifle. Someone was sniping at him.

Since he had often used such rifles himself, he knew their advantages and limitations. While the high muzzle velocity lent the bullet great range and accuracy, most models used a hand-operated, bolt-action breech mechanism. This reduced the rate of fire considerably compared to an automatic rifle or pistol.

The rifle was probably long and somewhat unwieldy, not designed for following a rapidly moving target. The field conditions weighed in Bolan's favor as well, since surrounding trees provided tremendous interference for long-distance shooting.

The series of conclusions flashed through his mind in a second. He decided that his best chance was to leap into motion the instant before the sound of the shot had faded from the woods.

Bolan zigzagged as he ran, making evasive turns as he scrambled from one patch of shrubbery to another.

Bullets sang around him in rapid succession, clipping leaves from the trees or thudding into trunks. Bolan counted every shot, since he knew that most sniper rifles held a maximum of ten rounds.

His senses were attuned to his opponent, and even as he ran he scanned his surroundings. His course directed him toward the sound of firing, which he estimated was near the right-of-way where he had entered the ravine.

He dodged behind a maple as another bullet whizzed around his shoulders. As he ducked behind a bush momentarily, Bolan spotted a muzzle-flash near the top of the path where he had descended. An excellent position, he remembered, with several large trees for cover and well screened from the road beyond.

The warrior's best defense was to continue his aggressive behavior. The closer he got, the more likely the gunman would be to turn and flee.

And then the Executioner would have him—provided the marksman didn't connect first.

Bolan raced through the sparse forest like a broken-field runner. Every step took him closer to a firing position where he could reply to the hidden gunner.

The shots came with increasing frequency as he neared the shooter's position.

Eight. Nine. Ten.

At the sound of the tenth round Bolan paused in his headlong run to steady himself against a tree trunk. If he had counted correctly, the assassin had used his entire magazine, and the warrior could afford to halt long enough to return fire.

He loosed a 3-round burst at the dark clump of brush where he had seen the telltale muzzle-flashes.

As soon as the last bullet had left the barrel, Bolan charged ahead on his erratic path. He grunted softly with the effort as he climbed the steep bank leading from the ravine in short, choppy steps. At the top of the bank he flopped down on the sharp grass and poked his head up above ground level.

About thirty yards away a four-wheel drive vehicle had driven onto the right-of-way nearly to the edge of the ravine. The driver kept low as he climbed out of the Jeep and bent over the wounded man. The sniper's arm and shoulder were covered in blood. Evidently Bolan's one short burst had caused more damage than the sniper's aimed fire, and the gunman's companion was attempting a pickup.

"Freeze!" Bolan shouted, interrupting the man in the act of hauling his fallen comrade into the back seat of the Jeep.

The man dropped his wounded friend and dived for the cover of the truck, drawing a pistol as he moved.

Bolan scooted sideways, firing as he ran.

The gunner under the truck answered with a machine pistol, swinging a line of fire rippling over the grass toward Bolan.

The Executioner found the range first, and the stream of bullets was choked off as a 9 mm slug from the Beretta caused the gunman to lose his grip on the weapon.

Bolan walked slowly over to the second man, the Beretta ready for any sudden tricks. A powerful Steyr SSG69 sniper rifle with a telescopic sight rested a few feet away.

The Executioner knew the gun well. The cold-hammered barrel, nearly twenty-six inches long, delivered rounds on target with bull's-eye accuracy. The dark green military stock was constructed entirely of plastic to prevent warping. A fine, precision rifle, but only as deadly as the man behind the gunsight.

"Congratulations," the wounded man grunted, grimacing around a thin mustache. "You're even better, more deadly than I was told."

"I want some answers," Bolan demanded. He judged that the man was in no danger of dying immediately, even though the shoulder wound looked painful.

"I'm sure you do. But I've got nothing to say. I never talk about my employers or myself. Professional pride, you know."

The sniper pulled his left hand from his pocket and laid it on his chest before he opened his hand. A fragmentation grenade sat in his palm, and the pin was missing.

Bolan didn't waste his breath cursing. The suicidal bastard wasn't going to take him out, too. The big man sprinted for the far side of the truck and continued running as the seconds counted down. He kept the body of the truck between him and the grenade as he powered over the grass, bending low.

Behind him, the grenade exploded with a fiery roar, igniting the truck in a secondary ball of flame.

The blast wave pushed Bolan sliding onto his face and hands as the concussion rode him down. A hot wind fanned his back and pieces of metal dropped nearby.

When the Executioner stood, he was relieved to discover that he'd survived intact except for a few minor scrapes. Behind him a black cloud boiled into the sky, marking the blast site for anyone who might care to investigate.

Bolan could hear the sirens wailing in the distance. It was definitely time to move out.

9

Bolan arrived back at his hotel with a course of action firmly in mind. He had decided there was no point in giving D'Angelo time to run or to improve his security.

At midnight he'd hit the criminal lair with everything he had. The warrior would rely on surprise and superior mobility to compensate for a disadvantage in numbers.

Bolan spent the next couple of hours checking his weapons and loading spare clips. He expected to use ammunition liberally to light the flames when it came time to fry D'Angelo once and for all.

Near midnight, he packed a gym bag with an assortment of guns and clips, as well as his combat webbing. He'd suit up in the ravine near D'Angelo's estate. He'd make his way from the opposite end of the gully this time, on the premise that the police would probably be covering the entrance he'd used earlier in the day.

The bag clanked faintly as Bolan rode the elevator down to the ground floor. When he emerged into the darkness of the outdoor parking lot, a woman's shrill scream broke the night.

Bolan dropped his bag by the Corvette and ran in the direction of the cry. He glanced at the lot attendant as he moved, noting that the man suddenly seemed totally absorbed in his tabloid.

All but one of his guns were back in the gym bag. However, the warrior had tucked the Beretta 93-R in its customary place and had sheathed a combat knife at his right ankle.

Bolan charged into the dim shadows at the rear of the lot, his battle instincts alert to potential danger. He almost stumbled over the body of a young woman who lay crumpled facedown on the ground.

He quickly scanned the area for any sign of an assailant. When he saw no one, he knelt beside the woman and turned her over. He felt her neck for a pulse, which beat under his fingers strong and steady. There were no visible bruises or lacerations to give a clue as to what had caused her to collapse.

The woman was a beauty, he noted, blond haired and fair skinned. A low-cut, clingy red dress showed a superb figure. Unadorned except for simple earrings and a tau cross around her neck, the woman needed no assistance from cosmetics. As he looked at her, her eyelids fluttered open. Sparkling blue eyes looked into his face from under long lashes.

"What happened?" she said in a low, rather husky voice.

"You tell me," Bolan replied.

"The last thing I remember," she said, propping herself up on her elbows, "I was struggling with my date. Now all I know is that I have an awful headache."

"You could have a concussion. You should see a doctor."

"No." She laid a hand on his arm in supplication. "I hate doctors. If it's all the same to you, I'd just as soon go back to my hotel and forget this ever happened. Would you drive me there please?"

Bolan found the appeal hard to resist. Obviously the woman had just gotten in way over her head. He figured that she was probably more embarrassed than hurt. "All right. Where's your car?"

"We came in his sedan, so I'm at your mercy. Could you give me a hand, please? I'm still a bit shaky. By the way, my name is Diana."

Bolan wrapped his arm around her slender waist. He could feel firm muscles under his hand as he helped her up and steadied her when she wavered on her feet momentarily.

He escorted her to his Corvette, extracted his keys and bent over the lock of the Corvette.

A premonition of danger made him turn a moment later, catching Diana in the act of pulling a long knife from a sheath strapped to her inner thigh. With a snarl that distorted her exquisite face, Diana drove the knife forward toward Bolan's stomach.

He dodged away, and the blade carved a line along the red paint of the car.

Diana didn't wait for a second try. She pulled the knife to her ear and let fly at Bolan's throat.

The warrior ducked then straightened to watch Diana running as fast as her long legs would carry her among the people on the sidewalks. He pulled the Beretta and gave chase. The woman had only a short lead, but Bolan couldn't risk a shot with so many people in the line of fire.

Diana reached out and pulled over a garbage can as she passed, tumbling it into Bolan's path. He tried to jump over it, but his foot slipped in something on the sidewalk as he leaped. Instead of clearing the obstacle he came down on the edge and rolled onto the dirty pavement.

He got to his feet almost immediately, but the fleeing woman had gained a few yards on him.

Changing tactics, Diana dashed into the traffic. A Datsun 280 ground to a halt inches from her and she ran to the driver's side, placing the vehicle between her and Bolan's gun.

As the driver shouted at her through his open window, she solved the getaway problem by opening the car door, judo-chopping the driver and dragging him onto the street. She jumped into the Datsun.

Bolan snapped two quick shots at the rapidly accelerating car. The rear window disappeared and one taillight went dark, but he didn't succeed in halting the speeding Datsun.

The warrior wasn't prepared to give up that easily.

Copying her trick, Bolan stopped the next car that came along, since he didn't have time to return for the Corvette. The pistol in his hand combined with a flash of a phony but official-looking ID in his hand persuaded the driver to yield his Honda Accord without any protest.

The big man steered for the receding taillights. He knew that if he let Diana escape, she would likely come gunning for him again. But next time it would be something more subtle but very deadly: C-4 under the dashboard, a long-range sniper shot or poison slipped into his food. Certainly the assassin wouldn't dare confront him face-to-face again. He was surprised that she had tried such a risky approach in the first place.

Bolan weaved through the sparse nighttime traffic, concentrating on narrowing the gap between himself and the single taillight ahead. Occasionally he steered into the oncoming lane to pass slow traffic, narrowly avoiding crashes through quick reflexes.

Ahead, Diana glanced in her rearview mirror and cursed her stupidity. Overconfidence had led her into trying the close kill, but she had badly underestimated her opponent.

Unfortunately she had developed a taste for killing, an unprofessional attitude that had tainted her objectivity. She derived far more satisfaction from a hands-on kill than a simple long-range shooting. In the past, whenever she decided that such an approach was feasible, the job had gone without a hitch.

Now the situation was reversed. She had become the hunted prey, and she couldn't seem to shake her pursuer. Another quick glance at the rearview showed the glowing eyes of Bolan's car creeping closer by the second.

Still, she had a few tricks yet to play. The big man wouldn't take her down without a fight.

Bolan hung on to her tail, following the Datsun around corners in a squeal of rubber and rushing through red lights heedless of oncoming traffic. Finally he managed to gain enough distance that he came to within a few car lengths of his attacker.

In a desperation move, Diana turned sharply left across two lanes of traffic and crashed the barrier of a multilevel parking garage.

The Honda fishtailed as Bolan jerked the wheel over hard, but he managed to keep the car under control. He barreled past the shouting lot attendant and up the ramp after the Datsun. If he gave her half a chance, Diana would abandon her vehicle and escape on foot, losing him among the stairwells and parked cars.

At the top of the sixth level, he discovered Diana's car blocking the ramp, the driver's door hanging open.

Bolan eased out of the Honda and edged to the back of the Datsun. The dimly lit parking garage showed no sign of the blonde, although she might be lying concealed ten yards away. He listened for sounds of running footsteps, but heard none.

The warrior broke cover and launched himself in a rolling dive for the tail of an Oldsmobile a few yards away. Shots echoed through the concrete garage as bullets whined off metal behind him. Obviously resourceful, Diana had managed to conceal a gun somewhere among her clothes.

Bolan had noted the direction the shots came from, somewhere among a line of cars deeper within the garage. He shifted along to his left, intent on flanking Diana's position and at the same time preventing her from reaching the stairwell.

When the Executioner prepared to duck around the last car in line before streaking up behind her, he dropped to the ground as he caught sight of long golden tresses a few cars away.

Diana had apparently grasped his plan immediately. She was an opponent he couldn't afford to misjudge.

Bolan crouched on the concrete and aimed the Beretta under the parked cars. Diana's position was partly hidden by the mass of tires, but the warrior only hoped to force her to break cover. He began to fire slowly, trying to ricochet the slugs under the cars to take a nip from the assassin's legs.

The hit woman didn't enjoy the new tactic. Her legs vanished as she slithered between several cars.

Bolan followed cautiously, since she turned to snap an accurate shot every once in a while. He guessed that she was heading for a second exit on the far side of the garage. The big man was happy to let her try to evade him that way. Once she reached the elevator door, she'd be dead if she tried to flee with the Executioner covering the escape route.

Diana realized her dilemma as she hid by the side of a car nearest to the elevator. An eight-foot gap stretched between the car and the door, and she would be exposed for long seconds before the elevator made its appearance. The lights of the city shone over the iron-and-concrete railing, and a vortex of empty cigarette cartons and other litter whirled in an eddy of wind.

To Bolan's dismay, the elevator slid open and a black youth walked out. Diana was on him like a tigress before Bolan could fire. She grabbed the unsuspecting teenager around the throat and held her pistol to the side of his head. "Nothing will happen to him, friend,'' she shouted, ''as long as you don't interfere with my getaway.''

For reply, Bolan blasted the elevator controls, sending a flurry of sparks flickering around the doorway. Because Diana was sheltered behind her hostage, it was impossible to shoot her without the chance that a final reflex would trigger a shot that would blow away the young man's brain.

''Any more tricks and I'll kill him,'' she yelled in rage.

They both knew it was an empty threat. Once the hostage died, Bolan would erase her in a moment.

''Give it up, Diana,'' Bolan said. ''Drop the gun and let him go.''

''No way.'' She began to back away, dragging the youth along in her strong grip. ''I'm a professional, and I'll end my career that way.''

With her back against the guardrail, Diana abruptly pushed the youth forward. With an easy, graceful movement she vaulted over the rail and into space.

10

Bolan steered away from the death scene as the warble of an ambulance sounded in the near distance. The paramedics wouldn't be able to do anything for Diana, or whoever she was.

The big man felt anger, directed partly at himself for being suckered in by a beautiful woman. Another part abhorred the sheer waste: a lovely woman, intelligent, charming—and a professional killer. Now she was nothing more than a spreading stain on the streets of Chicago.

Bolan turned his mind from the minor tragedy that had been played out minutes earlier. The woman had made her choice. It was her call.

He glanced at his watch, noting that the hands had crept close to three o'clock. Theoretically he could still hit D'Angelo's house before morning, but after considering the matter rationally, he decided it would be better to postpone the hit until the next day. D'Angelo's place would be a tough nut to crack, and Bolan had no inclination to give an edge to the Mafia hardmen by arriving on the scene already combat weary.

He decided against going back to his hotel. Clearly his cover had been blown, and there would likely be more company once Diana's death became common knowledge.

He stopped at a sprawling highway motel—picked purely at random—and waited in the lot for several minutes watching the traffic in case someone followed him in. When he was satisfied that he hadn't been tailed, he checked in with a sleepy attendant.

As the warrior stretched out on the bed he wondered where this mission was headed. He'd just have to shake D'Angelo's tree and see what fell to the ground. With the details of the next day's battle plan drifting through his mind, Bolan fell into a fitful sleep.

EVERYTHING HAD BEEN CHECKED twenty times over. Nothing remained to be done. Finally, as darkness fell, the Executioner decided to put the waiting to good use and take a position outside D'Angelo's compound. Any bit of data he might pick up in the final hours might prove useful.

For security reasons Bolan had rented another car, this time a silver-gray BMW 325. The luxury car fit in well with the posh surroundings of D'Angelo's respectable home turf of Oak Brook.

The big man cruised through the suburb but did a double take as a stretch limo passed him bound for Chicago. From the license plate, Bolan recognized it as D'Angelo's car.

As soon as the limo vanished around a curve, Bolan whipped the BMW around to follow. This changed his plans dramatically, since it would be far preferable to challenge D'Angelo when the don was away from his stronghold.

For all Bolan knew, the mobster might be bound for the airport, intent on fleeing the Executioner's deadly judgment.

If D'Angelo expected to escape, he was in for a very nasty surprise.

TONY D'ANGELO SAT in the back of the limo reading over his notes for the evening meeting. Two guards sat across from him, an unusual and intrusive reminder that he was very much in danger.

His chief capo had urged him to cancel the meeting and remain at the estate, where he could be effectively guarded, but D'Angelo had scorned the advice. This evening he was to meet with the chiefs of some of Chicago's most notorious gangs for the purpose of confirming and reviewing drug distribution operations.

If he failed to show, word would hit the street that he was scared, too frightened of a single man to show his face. And that wasn't good for business.

The mafioso knew that the end of his empire would be measured from that moment. The black gangs who ran the various neighborhoods feared nothing, death least of all. He'd lose their respect if they judged him a coward.

Without respect he would have nothing.

However, he'd sent a carload of enforcers ahead to guard the meeting hall. It would be their job to ensure his security, if such a thing were possible. In the meantime, his limo carried enough armor plate to withstand anything short of a rocket.

He'd been chilled to learn of Diana's death. She'd been reputed to be one of the top assassins in the country. If Bolan had bested her, what chance would a few simple Mafia soldiers have against him?

D'Angelo pushed the thought from his mind. He hadn't achieved his present lofty position by giving up easily. Bolan hadn't beaten him yet; with luck and skill he never would.

BOLAN FOLLOWED D'Angelo as the mobster cruised into Chicago's seedy side, separated from the mega-bucks corporations of the financial district by more than distance.

Thousands of residents lived in poverty among Chicago's South Side welfare complexes, only a few blocks from the yuppie enclaves along Lake Michigan's Gold Coast.

D'Angelo's driver steered for one of the worst areas along West Adams Street, deep in the heart of gang country. Every corner held moody, raucous collections of tough youths wearing the colors that marked their affiliation.

The lines between the Bloods, Vice Lords or Gangster Disciples were as clearly drawn as the Berlin Wall. Rival gang members straying into foreign territory risked certain injury or death.

Bolan slowed as though he were considering the provocatively clad hookers strolling the boulevard. He watched in his mirror as D'Angelo and four bodyguards hurried into the entrance of one of the high rises.

The big man drove rapidly into a more sedate neighborhood a few blocks away and parked where there was a better than even chance that the BMW would still be there when he returned.

When Bolan reached the housing complex he attracted a lot of hostile stares but no overt trouble. His size and menacing appearance served to keep the surly youths at a distance.

Five young hoods loitered in the main entrance smoking happy sticks—marijuana joints dipped in PCP or embalming fluid. They pretended to ignore the white intruder.

Bolan pushed through them, conscious of their dislike and suspicion. The only white people who usually visited the complex were police or social workers, and the big man didn't look like either one.

Inside, the building looked as if it stood one inspection away from being condemned. Occasional bare bulbs hung from a low ceiling. Holes had been punched in the walls at random, and what paint was still visible under almost continuous graffiti had turned a bilious shade of yellow. The halls smelled as though a decomposing body lay behind one of the apartment doors, and the noise of blaring televisions mingled with the wail of crying children and the occasional angry shout.

Bolan, hardened as he was to war and bloodshed, found it hard to connect this dingy slum with the America he knew and loved. The rot of the cities had spread deep and wide, dwelling side by side with luxury.

The big man wasn't a social critic, he was a warrior. He'd come to root out D'Angelo, no matter what dingy hole the man had crept into.

Bolan reasoned that D'Angelo wouldn't have come to this blighted neighborhood unless there had been a pressing business reason. That probably meant that a meeting was in progress with some of the gang members who controlled the street level distribution of the Family's drug operations.

His hand never far from the butt of the Beretta buried by his shoulder, Bolan wandered the halls cautiously, searching for some sort of meeting room.

He poked his head around the corner of one of the zigzag corridors and realized that he'd found his target. Outside a set of double doors, eight young men waited, each sporting gang insignia and a heavy firepower weapon. Fortunately they were so busy keeping an eye on one another that no one noticed Bolan's arrival.

The warrior retraced his steps, exiting through a side door into a parking lot crowded with rusting wrecks and a few burned-out hulks. The big man eased along the side of the building, counting paces until he felt sure that the next set of wide windows led into the meeting room. D'Angelo's caution hadn't extended to posting a guard outside the building.

Bolan peered cautiously through a small gap between a curtain and the edge of the window. About a dozen young thugs sat around a scarred U-shaped conference table. D'Angelo stood at the open end of the table, apparently lecturing his audience. The young blacks and Hispanics lounged back in their chairs with studied indifference, refusing to allow the mafioso to feel in control.

Bolan noticed, however, that three armed men in business suits were leaning against the wall. Undoubtedly more remained out of sight. The don wasn't so foolish as to trust his confederates' goodwill without enough security to squash any thought of armed opposition.

The warrior was forced to choose. He either backed away now and waited for a more opportune time with a still greater force opposing him at D'Angelo's home, or he faced a heavily armed gang at close quarters. He'd hold the element of surprise here, but that wouldn't serve him for long.

Bolan smiled grimly. He had a whole barrel of big fish collected, ready for a frying. The gang members inside were ruthless and brutal. He knew that tons of drugs flowed through their hands, sapping the little spare cash of some of the poorest people in the United States. Worse, their stoned customers, lost in apathy, forfeited any chance of ever escaping the lowest rung of poverty. Bolan had no doubt at all that many of these gang leaders' eager buyers would end up in prison, dead from an overdose or murdered in a soured drug deal.

The gang leaders required only a little experience and power to become as formidable as the don. The Executioner welcomed an opportunity to choke the savages off before they reached the big time.

Fortunately he had a bit of extra assistance in the form of a pair of fragmentation grenades.

Bolan checked his guns one last time. His head weapon would be a 9 mm mini-Uzi with 32-round boxes, ideal at close quarters. For backup, the Beretta and Desert Eagle rode in leather under a light jacket.

The Executioner popped the pins on the two grenades and flung the first through the window, aiming for a narrow gap in the center where the curtains didn't quite meet.

Shouts inside unnecessarily drew attention to the deadly metal canister, as it smashed the glass and tumbled into the room.

The warrior whipped the second grenade after the first and scrambled back to the shelter of the brick wall. A moment later the room vomited smoke and heat with a shrieking roar. Fragments of flesh and furniture rode the angry blast, screaming through the tattered remnants of the curtains.

Bolan waited for the second explosion, which drowned out a few wailing cries from skewered hardmen. He left his enemies no time to recover from the assault, executing a dive through the window and ending in a combat roll among the demolished furniture.

The room was nearly in darkness—the overhead fluorescent tubes hung shattered from the ceiling—but a faint glow spilled into the room from lights in the corridor. The exit door had been propelled off its hinges and lay splintered in the hall.

The big man evaluated the situation in one quick glance. Very little of the dingy furniture remained recognizable, let alone intact. The hardmen inside hadn't fared much better. Smoke and dust swirled in random eddies, half choking Bolan.

Sobs and shouts rose from shadowy corners, making the room seem like an annex of hell. Only one man was capable of firing at Bolan, and he got off a wild shot that vanished in the gloom before the warrior targeted the stunned man and took him out of play with a burst from the Uzi.

Bolan scanned the room for signs of D'Angelo, without success. He knew that the mafioso had been at the front end of the room when he'd let loose with the grenades, so the crime lord had either escaped or been blasted into fragments too small to be recognizable.

Suddenly the Executioner didn't have time to worry about the kingpin's whereabouts. The guards in the corridor began firing random bursts into the darkened room.

Bolan dropped to the floor, taking shelter behind a chunk of desk. He returned fire, scoring immediately on a black man in dark glasses and dreadlocks.

The Executioner fired rapidly, sighting every grouping. The guardians in the corridor popped into the doorway like targets in a shooting gallery, and the Executioner dropped them just as easily. When the gunfire from the hall slackened, he took to the offensive, bolting for the door with the Uzi held waist high in firing position.

Bolan swung around the doorway, his finger tightening on the trigger a fraction of a second before the last two guards could fire their weapons. The Executioner's blast weaved over them in a bloody stitchery, the gang members firing futilely into the walls and ceiling as they collapsed to the floor.

Bolan proceeded cautiously through the halls, conscious that an ambush might await him around any turn, but also mindful that every second that passed allowed D'Angelo a better head start. Bolan arrived at the front door without encountering any opposition. The hallways and common areas had magically cleared of people—the residents had wisely retreated to their apartments to wait out the fighting.

D'Angelo's limo had disappeared.

The Executioner trotted out the door and toward the quiet neighborhood where he'd stashed his car. He wouldn't press the pursuit at present. D'Angelo would be running for home, hoping to find safety in familiar surroundings. But Bolan wasn't about to let his quarry escape that easily. The Mafia godfather had bought himself a little time, but the Executioner had set the clock running. D'Angelo's final hours were counting down.

The mafioso owed a debt to society, and the Executioner intended to collect in full.

D'Angelo poured two fingers of Scotch into a crystal tumbler. His hands shook so badly that he spilled almost as much on the limo's carpeting. He polished off half in a swallow, the rest following a moment later.

Fortunately he was alone in the back seat. Only one of the guards he had brought with him had survived the attack and was riding shotgun in the front seat with the driver.

The thought of how near he had come to being killed sent D'Angelo reaching for the Scotch once more. Death had brushed by him in the past, but in recent years, since he had reached the pinnacle of success, it had been a distant, intellectual possibility.

Only an extraordinary sense of self-preservation had sent him running for the exit the moment the grenade had broken the window. He had stopped in midsentence and run, hardly conscious of what he was doing.

Because he had reacted when the rest had sat on their duffs, he was alive and they were dead.

He sat back in the luxurious seat and began to reflect on what had happened. The last thing he had expected was to be attacked in the middle of one of the toughest neighborhoods in America. This Pollock character obviously had guts to sneak up on him in the middle of gang territory and catch him by surprise.

Obviously his soldiers weren't capable of outgunning this deadly killer. The best assassin that money could buy had fallen victim to the mysterious big man. So it was up to him to outsmart Pollock if the Family was to be saved from destruction.

D'Angelo held out his hand and observed that he could now keep it flat and steady. He nodded, satisfied, and settled back in the seat. He imagined himself in his adversary's position. What would he do if he were Pollock?

Ideas tumbled through his head, but he reached no conclusions. The fact that the man had been able to track him to the meeting this evening proved that he had to be extremely lucky or have excellent sources of information.

Knowing what the man had accomplished thus far made D'Angelo think that he had it all. The only thing D'Angelo was certain of was that he would have a few surprises ready for the guy by this time tomorrow.

He'd guarantee that they wouldn't be pleasant.

11

The don looked at the ring of silent, somber faces and felt reassured. He had known some of these men for all his adult life. They had sworn the oath of loyalty and vowed to protect him as head of the Family—or die trying.

Fifteen good men, summoned via his car phone as he returned home, had assembled around him; a few more watched the grounds and monitored the security devices. Some twenty men in total, armed with hardware ranging from ancient but serviceable 9 mm pistols to modern assault rifles.

D'Angelo nodded his approval, satisfied with his force. He dismissed them with a few words of encouragement, sending them to posts scattered throughout the grounds. In a few minutes, every inch of the estate would be covered with fields of fire. He knew that his hardmen should be more than sufficient to keep Pollock at bay, or to blow away any man foolish enough to challenge a lion in its own den. But just in case, reinforcements were already on their way from around the state and from satellite operations as far away as Las Vegas and New York.

D'Angelo hoped that Pollock would strike, if only to give him the opportunity for revenge—and also to show his adversary who was the better man.

When the shooting was over, the don planned to do something horrible to the big man, alive or dead. He'd have to think of something so vile and memorable that the members of many Families would remember it for years.

D'Angelo leaned back in his easy chair and palmed a cigar. He scratched a match on shoe leather and began to puff. The subject of his nemesis's demise would provide him with a few minutes of pleasant contemplation.

The jitters had left him once he'd driven through the gates of his estate. His home was more than his castle, it was his fortress.

Suddenly the lights went out.

BOLAN EXAMINED D'Angelo's estate through the night-vision goggles, searching for any weaknesses that hadn't been apparent during his last inspection.

Electronic alarm wires were visible on top of the wall, and closed-circuit cameras covered a lot of territory. Spotlights shining from the roof and various banks scattered around the grounds illuminated every nook and cranny. The estate appeared almost as brightly lit as a prison yard—and about as difficult to cross undetected.

A short time ago, about a dozen men had poured from the house to take stations around the grounds. Bolan had noted each position within his range of sight. Most of the gunmen were too far away from one another to lend support if the going got tough. D'Angelo had spread his defenders far and wide in an attempt to cover the large estate. The Executioner knew that once he breached the defences, he could eliminate the scattered gunners one at a time.

The nearest man crouched by the pool cabana some fifty yards away. Another guard patrolled farther along by the side of one wing, while a third lay in a patch of shadow along the wall. Each could observe him the moment he set foot on the wall, even if the electronic alarms didn't sound the warning. Walkie-talkies blared at intervals as each gunman reported his position to a central coordinator.

Bolan believed that he'd spotted a weakness he could exploit: if he could destroy the power supply he could reach the house under cover of darkness, a condition that posed no problem for him, but would spook the opposition.

Bolan had driven directly to Oak Brook after retrieving his car and had trekked through the ravine to take up his position. He didn't want to risk allowing the mobster to slip away again.

Sooner or later, if Bolan kept pressing him, D'Angelo might decide to cut his losses and retire under an assumed name to someplace very quiet. It might not be exactly the time of his choice, but Bolan worried that the kingpin would decide he would rather live to spend some of his dirty money than wrestle with the Executioner. Forcing D'Angelo into a quiet rocking chair wasn't good enough. The mafioso deserved a much harsher sentence.

Bolan raised a special piece of weaponry to his shoulder and sighted on the point where the city power lines connected to the house, about 150 yards away.

The rifle was a Walther WA 2000 sniping rifle chambered for the .300 Winchester Magnum with a Schmidt & Bender variable power telescope mounted for sighting. The futuristic rifle was a complete departure from most designs. The entire weapon had been built around a special heavy barrel set into a rigid frame. The barrel was specially braced and fluted to resist vibration and harmonic effects as well as increase the cooling area. The bull-pup action delivered the recoil to Bolan's shoulder in a smooth, straight line through a stock that he had adjusted to his own fit.

Bolan squeezed softly after estimating for windage, and the lights winked out.

The warrior didn't take time to congratulate himself. Accurate shooting with a sniper's weapon was no more than what he expected of himself. Besides, he didn't have even a fraction of a second to waste.

A low babble of voices echoed from the far side of the wall as the hardmen called to one another in confusion. Bolan knew that with their eyes accustomed to the bright lights in the compound, they would be almost blind in the dark.

The warrior dropped from his perch, picked up the Uzi and jumped for the top of the wall, using a stump as a springboard. The barbed wire on top was no more than an annoyance to his tough combat gear. He paused for a heartbeat on the edge of the wall, then dropped noiselessly into D'Angelo's compound.

The Executioner could see the nearest guard standing in the door of the cabana, peering futilely into the dark. The man's rifle wavered at every noise, tracking hesitantly from side to side.

Bolan knew that in his nervous state the mobster might shoot at random at any moment. The Executioner forestalled that possibility by shifting the Uzi to his left hand and drawing the silenced Beretta as he ran. A 3-round grouping plowed into the hardman's chest, and he fell, dead, into the shadows of the cabana.

The big man trotted on, skirting the pool and making for the back door of the mansion. Just as he reached the steps, the backup generator kicked in, and the lights came alive. Faintly at first, and then more brightly, the house and yard burst into illumination. He had hoped for a little more time, but it had sufficed to breach the outer defense.

Now, like a boxer, he had dropped under his opponent's wild haymaker and prepared to deliver his own knockout punch.

Bolan flattened himself for a moment against the wall beside the steps. He felt exposed, for his dark gear contrasted starkly with the whitewashed walls of the house. However, the surveillance cameras pointed away from the house and directly toward the back door. The moment he put his foot on the back door landing, someone would know that he had arrived.

He glanced at the windowpanes nearest to him and noted that they were wired for alarms. D'Angelo clearly took no chances.

The faint blare of a walkie-talkie drifted from poolside, likely someone doing a head count by communicator. When the dead guard didn't respond, Bolan could expect some action.

Seconds later the back door popped open and two gunners raced out carrying submachine guns. They ran past Bolan without noticing him. But some inner alarm prompted one of the gunners to stop and look back toward the house, the other one turning to follow his comrade's lead.

That proved both men's undoing. The moment they turned in his direction, the Executioner unleashed the Uzi, 9 mm parabellum rounds playing over the hardmen in a figure eight. They dropped to the ground with piercing screams.

Bolan ran for the back door while echoes of gunfire still drifted around the grounds. He jerked it open with his finger ready on the trigger, half expecting to come face-to-face with reinforcements.

He entered the mansion unopposed and paused to lock the door behind him. He'd have plenty of exits to choose from when it came time to leave, and in the meantime he didn't want anyone sneaking up on him from the rear.

Bolan catfooted down a hallway, searching for the elusive don. The first door opened onto a small sitting room. Across the hall was a spacious kitchen equipped with banks of refrigerators and industrial ovens. D'Angelo obviously liked to entertain on a grand scale. The small room was probably for the servants, and now was luckily deserted.

Voices carried through the open door of the next room down the corridor, men calling back and forth as they tried to figure out what was going on. Bolan heard one announce that he was going to check for himself.

Bolan raised the Uzi in anticipation. When the gunman stepped into the hall, he erased the mafioso's look of shocked horror with a climbing burst before the guy had a chance to raise his Luger.

The warrior bounded over the body and whirled into the doorway. Two technicians sat by banks of monitors. Images of the grounds appeared and vanished monotonously, replaced by fresh views. The technicians were reaching for stubby SMGs that lay by the security boards.

The Executioner fired first before the gunners could track on target. He weaved the gun in a zigzag pattern over the hardmen until the Uzi clicked on empty.

The mafiosi tumbled to the floor, cored repeatedly by the steady stream of 9 mm death. Stray slugs impacted on the sensitive electrical gear, causing showers of sparks and rendering monitors and communications equipment inoperative.

Bolan paused to insert a fresh clip. Sparks had jumped from the electrical fires and raced up the curtains, setting off a smoke alarm in the ceiling.

With any luck, Bolan thought, in a few hours there would be nothing but ashes to mark the funeral pyre of the Mafia don.

D'ANGELO STARTED when the first sounds of shots reverberated from somewhere downstairs. He concluded in a flash that his nemesis had gotten onto the grounds when the lights went out.

He resisted the urge to run. In the first place, he could hardly expect his men to serve or defend him if he took off and left them to continue the battle. He'd lose their respect, and without respect a man had nothing. Besides, if Pollock dared to attack him in his own home, where in the world would he be safe? It was time to end the contest here and now.

There was also the practical consideration that unless he jumped out the window, he stood a chance of running into Pollock on the lower level. D'Angelo admitted to himself that he would be happy to avoid the confrontation under those circumstances.

He strode to the window and threw it open with a grunt. The guards nearby were still standing at their posts, although he was certain they must have heard the echo of shots even outside. They wouldn't think for themselves. That was why they needed a man like D'Angelo to guide them.

"Hey, Giancarlo," he called. The nearest man stood up straight and looked to him for orders. "Gather the men and get them into the house. But be careful. It sounds like Pollock's arrived."

The don walked over to a small cabinet, unlocked a drawer and removed a Browning Hi-Power 9 mm pistol. He checked the magazine and cocked the pistol in readiness. The gun had served his father well in World War II and in many deadly encounters afterward. D'Angelo had used it himself on more than one occasion when he had been in charge of collecting bad debts. It made a very satisfactory hole in any man who thought that he could cheat the Mafia out of what was owed.

He settled back in his easy chair and waited with the pistol focused on the open door. If Pollock made it this far, he'd learn that you couldn't count Tony D'Angelo out until someone threw the earth on his coffin.

D'Angelo repressed a cold thought that that day might arrive sooner than he expected.

BOLAN LISTENED at the heavy door that divided the service areas from the main part of the house. For the moment all seemed to be quiet.

He eased open the door and stepped into a broad dining room, entering a world of luxury far different than the Spartan functional areas. D'Angelo enjoyed his wealth and displayed it in old heavy furnishings, cabinets full of silver and crystal, and landscape paintings that smacked of old-master status.

Sliding double doors led into a spacious living room, furnished with overstuffed sofas and chairs. A wing ran off to the left, just beyond the main door of the house. Across from the entrance, a sweeping circular staircase climbed to the second floor.

Bolan had to hope that his quarry was still in hiding somewhere in the house. He couldn't cover all the exits, and if D'Angelo had chosen to run, there was nothing the warrior could do. However, his knowledge of the overbearing pride of Mafia dons told him that the crime kingpin wouldn't be driven from his home without a serious fight.

Outside, a shadow passed in front of a window, and Bolan dived to the floor.

The next instant the quiet was shattered. Gunners smashed the window with steady streams of fire that pocked the walls and kicked the stuffing from the chairs and sofas. Wood chips flew from walnut and mahogany furniture, and the few lights in the room blinked out one by one.

Bolan had found momentary safety tucked between a heavy chair and the wall—he could feel the chair tremble under the onslaught of high-velocity slugs.

The gunfire ended raggedly and Bolan hefted the Uzi, extracted a spare clip and drew the Beretta from its custom leather.

The gunmen poured into the house from all sides, a couple climbing through the demolished windows.

The Executioner concentrated first on the men who had charged through the front door. He fired two quick bursts, catching the hardmen in full flight. The Mafia gunners tumbled to the floor, screaming, blocking the entrance for anyone foolish enough to follow.

Bolan turned to a pair of men by the front window, who had landed rather heavily on the broken glass. He tagged them with a 3-round burst each, before they had a chance to get their bearings.

Slugs thumped into his chair and thudded dully into the wall behind him. He shifted his attention to a group of hit men gathered inside the dining room, shooting around the edges of the doors.

By this time the Executioner felt sure that he was in a clear combat zone. He reached for an inner pouch and grabbed a fragmentation grenade. He popped the pin and counted down two seconds before he lobbed it over the back of the chair.

A shout of alarm was followed by the sound of running feet. The exploding orb eliminated the frantic sounds of escape.

When the smoke cleared a little, the Executioner could see two bodies in the dining room. One lay by the rear door into the servants' quarters, while the other lay twisted under the window. Part of the ceiling had collapsed, and a small fire burned on the carpet, licking at the ruined furniture.

The other pair, with either faster reactions or more determination to elbow their way out, had made their escape. Bolan moved cautiously to the destroyed front window, knowing from his earlier observations that plenty of the enemy would still be alive.

Through tattered draperies he could see several men running as fast for the front gate as their feet would carry them. They had spent their courage in one brutal assault.

Bolan pressed on, scouting the rest of the main floor quickly and finding it deserted. He mounted the stairs slowly, alert for any sound of movement, or the cocking of a gun. The warrior now held the Desert Eagle in hand. For sheet stopping power it had few equals, and any encounter from this point on would be more likely to require one-shot destruction than a high rate of fire.

He reached the top of the stairs and began to work his way methodically through the upstairs rooms, each receiving a cautious scan. D'Angelo could be hiding almost anywhere, under a bed, behind a piece of furniture or in a closet.

In the game of hide-and-seek, the person hiding had a distinct advantage, since a bullet fired from a point-blank range was hard to evade.

Bolan stepped into a book-lined study and quickly looked around. The room appeared to be deserted just like the others. He paused at the doorway as he caught the scent of cigar smoke.

He turned and dropped in one fluid motion, the Desert Eagle seeking target acquisition.

A section of bookcase had been pushed noiselessly back, revealing a hidden room. D'Angelo's face snarled angrily over the Browning Hi-Power pistol.

The two men traded shots at the same instant, but it was hardly a fair trade. D'Angelo's shot whizzed harmlessly over Bolan's head, while the Desert Eagle's powerful Magnum slug caught the don square in the temple.

12

Bolan stepped over the remains of the once powerful Tony D'Angelo and into the hidden room.

The warrior was very much aware that there was a subplot to this mission that he had never quite been able to get an angle on. Why was D'Angelo so keen to obtain military secrets? Some of the answers to a host of questions might be hidden in the secret chamber D'Angelo had revealed in death.

Several filing cabinets lined one wall, and were fortunately unlocked. Bolan opened a drawer at random and pulled out a slim folder labeled with the name of a prominent state senator. The file held a number of documents, as well as photographs of the senator in a compromising position with two other people, one of them of his own sex. Blackmail had probably accounted for part of D'Angelo's seeming immunity to the law.

The wail of sirens and the rumble of heavy-duty engines penetrated to the small room. Bolan rushed out to the window, where he saw a small convoy of fire engines and police vehicles paused at the gate.

The warrior had run out of time. He took a few moments to stuff some files he had selected under his jacket and to push the bookcase back into position after dragging D'Angelo's body out of the hidden room. With luck the secret file room would stay hidden until Bolan chose to reveal its existence.

He dropped through the window and ran for the back wall as the emergency vehicles came to a stop by the front door. He slipped over the wall and vanished into the darkness.

A FEW MINUTES after showering off the grime and sweat of an evening of violence, Bolan sat and examined the files.

A file on Tom Clarkson contained enough data to put a CIA background check to shame. The entrepreneur's entire life was documented, from school grades and early girlfriends up to recent encounters arranged with hookers in D'Angelo's employ. A separate account listed the businessman's wins and losses at poker. Clarkson was nearly two million dollars in the hole and appeared to be losing ground fast.

No wonder D'Angelo had been able to call the shots.

The Clarkson Industries file listed transactions, presumably exchanges of information. But D'Angelo hadn't even trusted the security of his private files, since he had concealed the identity of whatever he was passing back and forth by the use of abbreviations.

One man or organization referred to as OD had been buying and selling, although D'Angelo had bought far more than he had sold. By contrast, someone identified only as V had paid enormous sums to the mobster. Many pieces of information had broken the half-million-dollar mark in price. On balance, it had been a very profitable business, netting the mafioso about thirty million dollars a year.

D'Angelo had been using Clarkson Industries as a source of information. What had been going on was clearer now—the mafioso had exploited Clarkson's entrée into the military arms industry to siphon off information for his own use.

The question that remained unanswered was who the other parties were. Was D'Angelo selling to other high-tech companies, the Japanese, the Russians or maybe even Khaddafi?

There were a lot more suspects than Bolan had time to chase down. At this point, he felt inclined to turn the problem over to Brognola and let the intelligence boys do the digging.

However, now that the immediate threat from D'Angelo had been eliminated, the case might sit gathering cobwebs on some petty official's desk at Langley.

Bolan decided that since he'd come this far, he'd push a little harder and see what gave. A call to Brognola would ensure that the warrior had access to D'Angelo's home.

THE NEXT DAY Bolan presented himself at the gate of the dead mafioso's estate. A uniformed officer, suspicious at first, finally waved him through.

The kitchen and security areas were smoldering ruins. Water had soaked the plush carpets, and smoke had discolored the light pastel of the walls. The house smelled like a drowned camp fire.

The numerous bodies Bolan had left scattered about the building had been removed. Upstairs in D'Angelo's study, the only trace of the former crime lord was a rusty brown stain on the Persian rug.

Bolan felt around the bookshelves for a few minutes before he found the latch to the secret compartment. Then he set about the task of examining the files, bypassing only the most obviously irrelevant.

From what he read, he gathered that a lot of powerful people across the country must be spending anxious hours wondering what would become of the information D'Angelo had been holding against them. When Brognola's people eventually examined the files, it might mean jail for some and embarrassment at the very least for others. But that was none of Bolan's concern.

When he finished with the last jacket several hours later, he had extracted only a little wheat from the chaff. The file on OD had contained only a phone number and a duplicate record of payments and receipts. D'Angelo hadn't put a single word on paper about the mysterious V.

However, Bolan did find something that he'd missed on his last visit—the mobster had an encryption device attached to a special telephone line.

The warrior knew that this wasn't standard office equipment. You couldn't walk into your local telephone company office and pick up a device usually associated with highly clandestine work.

Whatever dark, dirty work D'Angelo had been performing, he'd taken pains to keep inquisitive ears from listening in. Even a phone tap wouldn't harm him, since it was virtually impossible to descramble an intercepted message without the encryption key.

Bolan dialed Brognola and asked for information on the phone number, his one clue. A few minutes later the federal agent replied that the number rang a telephone in Phoenix, Arizona. He offered to have one of his men swing by and make a few discreet inquiries.

An hour later Brognola delivered word that the address of the phone number in Arizona was a small office that contained a telephone and answering machine and nothing more. The person who had rented the office had paid five years' rent in advance in cash. Brognola promised to keep digging, but he didn't expect much.

Bolan had seen that kind of blind before. Someone anywhere in the world could retrieve messages from the answering machine and never have to set foot in the office.

Dead end.

The big man had one other possibility. He could ring the number and leave a message. He knew enough about D'Angelo's operation that he might be able to bluff for a while. However, considering that this would be his one chance, he decided to try another play first.

Bolan drove into the center of the city and rode the elevator to the top of a giant skyscraper, stopping at an innocuous doorway labeled MC Consulting. He pushed through the door and barged past the secretary, ignoring her insistence that Mr. Conway was in a meeting.

Lucas Conway made his living operating on the shadowy fringes of espionage. No one had ever pinned anything on the information dealer and made it stick.

The man was hunched over a conference table with a waxy-complexioned individual who could have been a Latin American. Both men turned to glare at Bolan.

"What do *you* want? You should have called first instead of interrupting a very important meeting." Bolan could hear both anger and anxiety in Conway's tone.

"Somehow I think you would have been unavailable if I had called." Bolan locked eyes on the customer, and he gestured over his shoulder toward the door. "Take a hike."

"How dare you?" The man stood and hissed in a voice heavily laden with a Spanish accent, "No lesser man gives me orders."

Bolan stepped forward, prepared to urge him out of the office. The man reached under his jacket, searching for gunmetal.

The warrior chopped down with a stiffened hand. Bones crunched under the impact, and a 9 mm Browning pistol dropped to the carpet. The customer uttered a strangled yell.

Bolan took him by the good arm and ushered him out to the secretary. "This man hurt his arm, so look after him, would you?"

The secretary's eyes flickered to her boss, who stood behind Bolan. Conway nodded and the pair left.

"I came out on the short end of the stick the last time we were thrown together. What do you want, Bolan?" Conway asked warily.

"Information. What do the initials *OD* mean to you?"

"Overdrawn, officer of the day, on demand, overdose, doctor of optometry. How do those grab you?"

Bolan could detect a note of tension beneath the levity. He leaned forward in his chair. "Cut the crap."

"All right. Give me a context." Conway was short and nearly bald. He favored loud ties and pungent after-shave. He had never forgotten a thing he'd heard, read or seen in his entire life.

"How about military intelligence, especially dealing with advanced electronics?"

"You don't mean the Old Dogs, do you?" Conway said with a rush.

Bolan was intrigued. "Tell me about them," he demanded.

The intel broker lowered his voice automatically, as though afraid of being overheard. "The Old Dogs are rumored to be a group of former engineering wizards who have banded together to gather and share knowledge about military electronics. Most of them worked on the government's 'black' projects, so secret that even the Secretary of Defense is briefed on a strictly need-to-know basis. They are thought to know every detail of the innards of weapons systems ranging from the Stealth bomber to cruise missile inertial guidance systems. However, their specialty is electronic warfare and countermeasures."

Bolan could imagine how valuable that kind of information would be—and how dangerous it would be to Western security if it fell into the wrong hands.

"Why haven't I heard of this group before?" he asked.

The other man laughed cynically. "Let's just say they're very shy and secretive. I imagine that the intelligence community knows of their existence, although the size and composition of their membership is quite speculative."

"What kind of service do they provide?"

"A simple matter of exchange. They'll divulge secret details of government contracts and the occasional technical tidbit in return for a sizable payment."

"I suppose you know how to get hold of them," Bolan said dryly.

"That piece of knowledge has been useful to me from time to time," Conway admitted.

"Then tell me."

Conway sat back in his chair. "You're asking me to just give away a very valuable piece of information, part of my livelihood. Is that fair?"

"No, but you're going to tell me just the same."

"You'll owe me for this if I tell you," Conway said unhappily.

Bolan remained silent.

"All right," the small man growled. He gave Bolan a coded message that he'd have to place on the Phoenix answering machine. "If the Old Dogs haven't phoned you within twenty-four hours, you won't hear from them. They'll check pretty thoroughly, so in addition to a pile of cash you better have a solid cover and a good reasons for calling. If they get the slightest bit suspicious, they'll bury themselves for a few months and pull the hole in after them.''

The big man left the office feeling confident that he had found at least one answer to the mound of questions that had been piling up since the start of this mission. He was determined to find out to what extent the Old Dogs were involved in the D'Angelo-Clarkson connection. To do that he would need a believable ally. Fortunately he had one in his pocket, one who would be happy to cooperate.

Bolan would make sure of it.

''WELL, WHAT'S on your mind?'' Colonel Valeri Lyalin barked at his assistant, who had been lingering in front of the senior officer's desk in a way that indicated he had something to say, but hesitated to bring it out. There was good reason for Captain Karkov's reluctance. The colonel could be brutal.

There was no holding back under the colonel's fierce gaze. ''It's that business with D'Angelo. His death makes me wonder if we should abandon our program and leave while we can,'' the young captain said.

''Your reasons?''

''Our mission has been a great success. We shouldn't jeopardize it by assuming needless risks.''

''You think that I'm risking our project foolishly?'' The colonel's eyes glittered like black diamonds in the soft light.

Karkov swallowed hard to ease his constricted throat. ''D'Angelo was destroyed by a powerful enemy. Who knows what further havoc he could wreak?"

Colonel Lyalin watched his subordinate carefully, silently. The assistant began to feel like a rabbit mesmerized by a snake.

"In the first place," the colonel finally said, "it's not for me to say when our mission has been completed. I'm at the mercy of my superiors. In the second, I don't believe that any one man could be a threat to us."

Captain Karkov listened but looked unconvinced.

"However," the colonel continued, "I believe in caution. Prepare for us to move tomorrow to a new headquarters, and to place all possible areas of contact under surveillance. We won't be caught unprepared."

Karkov clicked his heels and backed out of the office, amazed that the colonel had taken his suggestion so well. Colonel Lyalin must be even smarter than he'd thought.

TOM CLARKSON LOOKED UP gloomily when Bolan entered the small cell-like room that he'd been given, pending a more permanent arrangement. The once powerful industrialist had yet to come to terms with the fact that he was a prisoner of the state. Clarkson knew that he could very well spend the declining years of his life in surroundings limited by barbed wire and concrete unless he gave the Feds everything they wanted.

"What do you want?" he asked sourly.

"You asked me a while back what you could do for me in repayment for my getting your wife away from D'Angelo. I'm here to collect," Bolan said.

Clarkson snorted and turned to the wall. "If it hadn't been for you, I wouldn't be in this mess. And you expect me to help you? Forget it!"

So Clarkson had changed his tune. Bolan wasn't surprised. Incarceration didn't bring out the best in people, especially the weak ones.

"You either help me or you'll find yourself doing hard time with criminals who make D'Angelo look like your fairy godmother."

Clarkson swung around. "In your dreams," he sneered. "The Feds need me to bring down D'Angelo. They'll give me what I want, including the federal witness protection program."

"I wouldn't count on it. D'Angelo's dead."

The industrialist gaped at Bolan. "You're not serious!"

Bolan nodded. Both men knew that the situation had changed irreversibly. Clarkson was now expendable, his information useless.

Prison would be bad, but freedom would be worse. Clarkson wouldn't last very long if D'Angelo's associates decided that he'd been in any way responsible for the don's death.

Clarkson looked at Bolan with hatred in his eyes. The industrialist had managed to distort the facts so that he believed that it was Bolan rather than he who was to blame for his swift and dramatic fall from wealth. "What do I have to do?" he asked, the words tasting like bile in his throat.

"It's easy enough. You just have to be yourself."

13

Bolan knew that he was being watched.

The sun probed his back with warm fingers as he sat in an outdoor café in Denver, Colorado, waiting for some mysterious contact to make his move. Clarkson sat across the white metal table, morose and silent. The eyes of both men were hidden behind aviator sunglasses to guard against the strong mountain sunshine.

Clarkson had thrown out the bait. He had left a message on the Old Dogs' answering machine requesting a meet. The story was that now that D'Angelo was out of the picture, the industrialist preferred to deal directly.

The secretive network had responded twelve hours later, and arranged a meet for the following day. Bolan and Clarkson had taken a shuddering military transport to the city. The warrior had appreciated the lift, since his bags full of military hardware wouldn't have passed even the most cursory airport security check.

Now they sat and waited, Bolan impatient for events to kick into gear. He glanced around surreptitiously, as though searching for the waitress. A scattering of patrons occupied other tables, but nothing about any

of them aroused his suspicions. However, a good surveillance person strove to be unobtrusive, and anyone
there, from the flaxen-haired college student poring
over her chemistry book to the blue-haired old lady
delicately sipping her tea in the corner, could be a
plant.

Bolan had reviewed that lesson once already on this
mission, thanks to the beautiful assassin Diana.

A waiter approached carrying a portable telephone, which he handed to Clarkson. The entrepreneur listened briefly before hanging up the receiver.
"Come on," he said to Bolan. "We have to be across
town in twenty minutes."

Clarkson gave Bolan directions as the big man
climbed behind the wheel of the black Lincoln they
had rented on arrival. To keep up appearances,
Clarkson got into the back seat. A few minutes later,
they were in front of a drive-in soda stand.

Once again, there were plenty of nondescript people milling around. Bolan and Clarkson leaned against
the side of the Lincoln until a telephone rang in a
nearby booth. Clarkson hurried to answer it.

A few minutes later they parked in the lot of a suburban mall near a hamburger joint. A third telephone
call sent them driving out of town, climbing steadily
upward through the foothills leading to the little town
of Evergreen. Mount Evans, one of the highest in
continental America, dominated the landscape.

Their directions were sufficiently detailed that Bolan believed the Old Dogs were finally satisfied that no
dirty tricks were planned.

A few miles outside Denver Bolan steered down a secondary route leading into the mountains. The cracked and potholed pavement showed signs of only occasional use. When they arrived at the rendezvous, an abandoned dry goods store in the middle of a ring of trees, a white pickup awaited them.

The wind whispered among the pines, and birds chirped and screeched in the trees. A note slipped under a windshield wiper directed them to leave their car and take the pickup provided for the remainder of the trip.

Bolan complied reluctantly. Presumably the mastermind behind all the precautions wanted to prevent them from bringing along any transmitters or other hidden surprises.

The warrior contented himself with the Beretta tucked under his arm, regretfully leaving the trunk of the Lincoln packed with arms and ammunition. No doubt some of the unseen operatives of the Old Dogs would be picking over his goods the moment he drove out of sight.

Following the directions on the rough map that Clarkson had drawn, Bolan turned off the road onto a twisting rutted path that led among the pines. Moments later the truck burst through the trees. A small cabin stood in a clearing, poised at the edge of a sheer cliff.

A man stood on the porch clad in a red hunting jacket. He waved and beckoned them from the truck.

Bolan and Clarkson approached cautiously. The warrior was aware that a dozen men could be hidden undetected within the dark ring of trees.

"Come on in," the man said, holding open a screen door. "I'm Joe Smith. Either of you guys want a beer?"

Bolan and Clarkson both refused. This was the last kind of reception Bolan had expected. Their host was around thirty-five, a little above average height but very stocky and clad in a flannel shirt and faded jeans. Smith looked more like a truck driver than an electronics wizard.

Smith stopped Clarkson at the door. "Got your admission ticket?" he asked.

Clarkson wordlessly passed over the briefcase he'd been carrying. It contained a half million dollars, the Old Dogs' price for a meeting. Bolan had gotten Clarkson to authorize the withdrawal from his company's accounts—far better that they be used than frozen indefinitely once the federal investigation began in earnest.

Smith stepped in after them and threw the briefcase onto a rocking chair. He told them to go through to the veranda on the other side.

The view was spectacular. The veranda had been built over the edge of the cliff, and a swift mountain stream glittered at the bottom of a valley two thousand feet below. A vista of mountains and forest stretched into a hazy horizon. Large birds wheeled and dived on the air currents far below the ledge.

"This is God's country," Smith said admiringly as he joined them. "Now, what did you boys want to talk about so badly?"

"Is this the whole meeting? Is this what we paid a half million for?" Bolan asked.

Smith looked at him consideringly. "This is all you'll get of a meeting unless I decide that you deserve to meet the rest of the selection committee. The half million was good-faith money, nothing more. Call it an application fee. There'll be plenty more asked of you in future—if you're allowed to join."

Clarkson launched into a long, prepared explanation of how D'Angelo's death had left him out on a limb. The don had told him of the contact with the Old Dogs and how valuable their information had been for procuring contracts. Clarkson didn't want to let the connection drop.

"I see," Smith said doubtfully. "If that's all you wanted, why bring along a gorilla and half an arsenal in the trunk of your car?"

"This gentleman is my new bodyguard. With all of the problems recently in Chicago, I thought it in my best interests to hire a little protection."

"Well, you and your muscle man had better know that there are a lot of wild areas in these parts." Smith spoke conversationally, as though discussing yesterday's baseball. "Why, if you were to go missing around here, it's unlikely that anyone would ever find your bodies. If they did, the coyotes and buzzards wouldn't leave two bones together. Keep that in mind if you think of getting rough—or plan on selling us out."

"I won't forget it," Bolan said. He made it sound like a challenge. Clarkson, on the other hand, looked a little green, evidently imagining his body strewn over the hillside in bloody pieces and gnawed by wild animals.

Bolan locked eyes with Clarkson, and the industrialist got the message.

"One thing I won't put up with is sabotage," Clarkson said, mustering a tone of indignation. "I found out that D'Angelo was paying men to pass components that were defective and to fake test results on prototypes. God knows what sort of trouble that will cause in future, but I won't put up with it anymore."

Smith frowned in apparent puzzlement. "I don't know about D'Angelo's private dealings," Smith said, "but the Old Dogs don't approve of anything that would injure the United States. We're a very patriotic group. After all, what could be more American than making lots of money? But we would never approve of either sabotage or selling information from those godless, untrustworthy Commies. So rest your mind on that score, Clarkson."

The man was either an excellent actor or he was speaking the truth. Bolan believed Smith's denial.

Their business concluded for the moment, Bolan drove them back to the exchange point in the pickup. Smith, if that was his name, had told them that they would be contacted at their hotel that evening.

The big man felt content at the afternoon's work and confident that it would bear fruit later in the day. Clarkson had handled himself well, better than Bolan had dared hope. The possibility that the entrepreneur would dissolve under the pressure had nagged at Bolan.

The warrior concentrated on the task at hand, steering along the twisting mountain highways. This campaign, like so many others, reminded him of a baseball pitch—first the choosing of the pitch, then the deliberate, almost ritualistic motions and the setting of the pitching stance. Finally the windup, starting slowly but terminating in the controlled energy that sent a baseball nipping the corner at more than ninety miles an hour.

Another inning had begun. Soon it would be time to deliver the final strikeout and send the Old Dogs to the showers.

"THERE IS BAD NEWS, Colonel."

Colonel Valeri Lyalin didn't read bad news on his assistant's face. Rather, Captain Karkov glowed with suppressed excitement. That could only mean that he felt that his theory about imminent danger had been vindicated. "You have a report of Bolan in the area," the colonel said simply.

The assistant's face fell, robbed of the surprise value of his message. "That is so, Colonel. He has been spotted in Denver."

"And have you any idea of his purpose here?"

Karkov spread his hands. "I contacted a source in Chicago named Conway. He sold me the information that he had put Mack Bolan onto the Old Dogs. That would account for his presence in the city. However, it is possible that he lied."

The colonel thought for a moment. Conway had occasionally provided a morsel of useful data, but did that justify his existence? Did Conway suspect whom he was truly dealing with? Could the informant be trusted?

The answer to the last question was a definite no, which made the other questions irrelevant under the circumstances.

"Send two men to pick up Conway. Find out if he actually sent Bolan here on our trail. Then terminate him."

Karkov backed away to execute his order.

The next problem was what to do about Bolan and the Old Dogs. Lyalin had tried in the past to infiltrate the intelligence organization and had failed miserably. He had little more knowledge of its membership or resources than when he started investigating them.

Colonel Lyalin decided in a fit of pique that if he couldn't have the information that the Old Dogs possessed, then no one else should either.

As an officer in the KGB, his orders were clear: protect the security of Mother Russia and of the Communist Party in particular. As the officer in charge of the Western branch of Directorate T of the First Chief Directorate, his responsibilities centered on the collection of scientific and technological intelligence. His assistant, however, was an officer of the Eighth Department of Directorate S, responsible for assassination and sabotage, or as his officers sometimes called it, "wet work."

Secrecy was paramount. In this age of *glasnost*, it would never do to have his operation fingered by American intelligence. He would find himself transferred to the Border Guards, manning a security post on the Arctic Circle instead of living a comfortable life in the decadent democracies of North America.

It was time to unleash his young assistant on the unsuspecting Bolan.

CLARKSON JUMPED when the telephone rang. He picked it up on the second ring and listened carefully. "A car will be waiting for us in fifteen minutes outside the hotel," he reported to Bolan.

Bolan grunted. At last the waiting was over. The two men had rehearsed Clarkson's part many times, and the industrialist would do just fine—unless the Old Dogs took the precaution of truth drugs or hypnosis or some other form of inquisition that delved below the conscious mind.

In that case they were likely both dead men.

The strain was beginning to tell on Clarkson. His face looked pinched, his eyes those of a man twenty years older. Building a company, fighting with unions and battling for contracts hadn't prepared him for risking life and limb.

A few minutes later the pair climbed into the back seat of a dark blue limo. The windows in the back seat were blacked out, and the electronic window controls wouldn't function. Bolan wished that he had the reassuring weight of the Beretta 93-R nestled into his shoulder, but a thorough search before he was allowed into the car had relieved him of his weapon. Clarkson carried a briefcase containing another half million.

The limo turned frequently, disrupting Bolan's sense of direction. The drive lasted a half hour, but for all he knew, they might have returned to their point of origin.

At long last, the back door opened and the two men climbed out. They'd been driven into a three-car garage, and the door was drawn shut behind them, giving no clue as to their location.

The chauffeur led them through a door and into a functional meeting room. "Mr. Clarkson and his associate," the driver announced.

Bolan saw that six men, including the man called Smith they'd met earlier, were sitting in armchairs around a table. Each was dressed in comfortable clothes, and most had mugs of beer in front of them. A large plate of nachos and cheese, half-consumed, occupied the center of the table.

The men seemed relaxed, informal, unassuming, hardly a group capable of manipulating and subverting the most secretive and advanced industries of the most powerful nation on earth. Bolan was surprised.

"Not much to look at, I expect you're thinking," Smith said. "We look like we could hardly balance a checkbook, let alone design a weapons system. We like money and beer, not business suits and fancy French wines. But every one of us has a doctorate in electrical engineering, and we're smart enough to have friends in every high-tech company in the U.S. of A."

Smith nodded to the chauffeur. "Escort Mr. Clarkson's associate into the kitchen and get him whatever he wants. We have things to discuss."

Bolan had expected this to happen. It was up to Clarkson to gather whatever information he could while Bolan looked for clues to their whereabouts and plotted strategies to destroy the Old Dogs.

The driver led him into the kitchen and turned on the television, tuning into a baseball game. Bolan figured on a few minutes to let the driver get absorbed in the game, and then he would slip away, ostensibly to the washroom. He'd have an opportunity to explore the house in preparation for another, more violent visit.

He took a beer from the driver and had a short swallow. A few minutes later he excused himself.

CAPTAIN KARKOV CROUCHED in the grass with a Carl Gustaf gun, adjusting the luminous front and rear adaptors on the telescopic sight. He was conscious of Sergeant Popovich hovering by his shoulder as though he intended to snatch the launch tube from his hands instead of loading rounds in the breach. The sergeant didn't much like him, but Karkov didn't give a damn. He outranked Popovich, even though the NCO was twenty years his senior and a veteran of the horrific Afghanistan campaign to boot.

The killing machine swiveled easily on its tripod as he sighted through the telescope on the house two hundred yards away. He found it more than a little ironic that he would be using a NATO weapon to annihilate enemies of the U.S.S.R.

The device was technically a light antiarmor weapon, designed to destroy main battle tanks. The punch came from a rocket-propelled, fin-stablized high-explosive antitank projectile capable of cleaving through titanium steel.

However, it was also capable of firing high-explosive rounds, which should make quite an impression on the stone building that had become his target.

The mission so far had been executed faultlessly. No less than a dozen cars had been used to tail the limousine to its destination to minimize the likelihood that anyone would notice that the vehicle was being followed.

Now Karkov and seven men, including the troublesome Popovich, planned to terminate what would be the final meeting of the Old Dogs. Each member of the KGB contingent carried an Uzi for consistency, easily purchased in a black market deal.

Fortunately the meeting place lay beyond the edge of town, in a quiet, rural area that was unlikely to be disturbed for some time to come.

The bloodshed had already started. Moments ago five perimeter guards had been discovered patrolling the grounds and had been ruthlessly eliminated by Karkov's men. Three of the team had silently rejoined Karkov at the rendezvous, while the other three had spread out in case any more guards put in a belated appearance. They would also cover the other entrances in case anyone escaped the main assault.

The captain had orders to make sure that there were no survivors, and he intended to carry out these orders to the letter.

By day he and his men maintained a quiet position in the community, working as traveling salesmen or businessmen in the import-export trade. Each had been carefully smuggled into the country, supplied with his own "legend," a carefully crafted identity. Now it was time to revert to an identity that surfaced only on convoluted trips behind the Iron Curtain for training and briefings.

Karkov and his men had been trained among the cream of the commando service. Nothing but success was acceptable.

Now he steadied the Carl Gustaf until the cross hairs aligned on a single curtained window.

14

Bolan was a little surprised at the ease with which he was able to slip away. He could have knocked the guard unconscious and disappeared, but he wanted to minimize the risk of arousing hostilities with Clarkson caught in the middle. The warrior hoped to make a quick soft probe, in and out before anyone missed him.

However, he was virtually unarmed. Only some plastic looped around his waist and a sharp, flexible blade tucked into his belt had escaped the search before he and Clarkson got in the Old Dogs' limousine. But events had a way of following their own course. Bolan would deal effectively with whatever came his way.

He pushed through the exit from the kitchen area into the remainder of the house and waded into trouble, seeing at once why the guard had been so casual about his movements. Two men blocked the doorway, each looking as if he could have competed successfully for the big money on the pro wrestling circuit. One man held a pistol half-buried in his huge paw.

Thoughts flashed through the warrior's mind in swift succession. If he played hardball, outnumbered at least three to one, he'd be committing himself to fighting his way out with Clarkson. If he backed down, he might miss his only opportunity to stop the Old Dogs.

The Executioner was a man of action.

Bolan stared at the guards a moment, then turned away, lashing back with one heavy boot and catching the man with the gun a solid crack on the hand.

The big gunner grunted in sudden pain, and the pistol tumbled from his grasp, skidding under a low stand.

Bolan pressed home his attack, slugging the second man with a powerful jab to the jaw. The blow would have sent a lesser man sliding into dreamland, but his bulky opponent just staggered back a step and shook his head.

The warrior followed with a jab to the face, a blow that spread the hardman's ample nose across his face. The guy stumbled back, tripped over his feet and crashed into a long table.

Bolan put his weight behind a tall china cabinet, toppling it onto the man lying among the broken pieces of the wrecked table.

The wounded man finally decided to get back into the action, after having given up trying to retrieve his gun. He charged Bolan with a howl, hugging his injured wrist protectively against his chest.

The warrior stepped aside from the massive brute's shambling rush, sticking out his foot as he evaded the man's clawing hands.

The fighter tripped and lost his footing, a hard shove in the back added for good measure. The guy plunged forward like an out-of-control truck until he slammed headfirst into the wall.

First round to the Executioner, on falls.

But the two guards proved only the first and weakest link of defense. The sounds of smashing furniture had attracted the driver from his ball game. The Executioner turned to find him standing in the doorway to the kitchen, a Heckler & Koch MP-5K submachine gun leveled in front of him.

Bolan whirled again as he heard more men shuffle into position, blocking the doorway from the dining room into the rest of the house. Each toted a pistol.

The warrior was surrounded, outnumbered and outgunned.

Suddenly the roof fell in with a roar.

KARKOV WHOOPED in excitement as the projectile crashed home. The target window vomited a great gout of flame, and bricks and mortar rode the shock wave.

The Russian swung the Carl Gustaf and aimed it at a window near the other end of the house, where a glimmer of light showed. It was only good tactics to use superior firepower to neutralize the opposition before his men mopped up. Popovich tapped him on the shoulder, and he squeezed the trigger and blew apart the far end of the building. He fired once more, and the central core of the brick house, weakened by the explosive pounding, collapsed into a pile of rubble.

It had taken only thirty seconds to demolish the spacious house. While parts still stood intact, the bulk of the dwelling had dissolved into fragmented brick. Fires burned out of control, promising to reduce whatever combustible material remained to blackened cinders.

It would be a miracle if anyone had survived.

Just in case, Karkov's men were tightening their grip, closing the ring of death around the ruins to ensure that no one survived.

Karkov dropped the launch tube and gripped his Uzi. The weapon, he'd been assured, was completely sanitized and untraceable. However, he'd personally collect it later. The Americans knew him as Jim Robbins, dealer in international antiques. It was a life he thoroughly enjoyed, and he'd take every precaution necessary to retain his privileges.

The chatter of a submachine gun penetrated the crackle of flames, and Karkov moved a little faster.

There was killing still to be done.

THE FIRST EXPLOSION catapulted the driver through the doorway onto the broken dining room table, where he lay shattered, his back flayed to the bone.

Bolan was on the move. As plaster fell from the ceiling and the walls quivered, he bolted for the shelter of a sturdy wardrobe. Swirling plaster dust filled his lungs with every breath. The lights had vanished, plunging the room into a gloom lit only by the flicker of flames from the burning conference area and a soft glow backlighting the Old Dogs' hardmen.

There was a chance that the gunners would chase him down before he could flee from the dining room. However, the only viable exit was through what had been a heavily curtained window. The glass had shattered under the blast pressure, and the curtains flapped in tattered fragments. But enough of the frame had stayed intact to make getting out a matter of a few moments' work.

The guards might be slightly stunned from the explosion, but they could hardly fail to miss as he lingered by the window.

A second explosion rocked the house, resounding from the far wing. The floor shifted, and a jagged section of ceiling dropped with crushing force. The gunmen fled.

Bolan waited only a second before he made his move. The warrior first had to determine whether Clarkson was still alive.

Heat assaulted his face as he plunged into the smoke-filled burning kitchen. He broke into a sweat, and beads of the salty liquid rolled into his eyes along with coils of stinging smoke.

The front part of the house had collapsed, and through the smoke Bolan thought he saw figures outside.

He moved with an urgency made more potent by the knowledge that somewhere in the dark men waited, intending to kill anything that moved—after they'd brought the house down.

To punctuate the thought, the house quivered as another explosion dug into walls and masonry. With a roar that shook Bolan to his knees, the second story collapsed, covering him with plaster dust.

Bolan rose, climbed over a fallen cross beam then headed down the corridor that led to the meeting room.

Smoke choked his lungs, but over the acrid smell of blazing wood came a more penetrating smell: the sweet reek of burning flesh.

He reached the conference room. Among the demolished furniture, the Old Dogs lay strewn in pieces like sections of meat in a butcher shop. Clarkson lay facedown near the door, intact but dead.

Bolan turned away, distressed that the entrepreneur had come to such a bad end. Tom Clarkson was no innocent, but Bolan had asked for his help. The warrior hadn't planned it to turn out this way. However, living large sometimes meant taking risks. From time to time, in spite of careful planning and meticulous preparation, the bad guys got in a good shot. It was a shame that Clarkson had paid the price, but he had started down the path to destruction many years ago.

Bolan believed that everyone had to take responsibility for his own actions. He refused to allow for a free ride. The apologies of criminals who claimed that they were evil because they hadn't had a choice didn't move him one inch.

He retraced his steps through the inferno to the kitchen, which was barely passable. A ring of flame separated him from the outside wall, which had caved in under the force of the explosion. Bolan threaded his way through burning debris to the back window. Smoke filled his lungs and particles of black cinders stung his eyes.

He broke away an aluminum strut blocking the window and climbed through onto a marbled patio, then froze by the edge of the foundation, watching muzzle-flashes in the near distance and hearing the sharp chatter of a submachine gun.

Bolan gasped clean air into his oxygen-starved lungs, then shucked off his jacket and tie while his eyes grew accustomed to the darkness. The burning house cast wavering shadows, occasionally illuminating one of the gunmen who stood watching the funeral pyre.

Bolan edged forward to a low stone wall that enclosed the patio, and peered around a large urn balanced on a post. To the left, two attackers were exchanging fire with a single gunman crouched by a large piece of lawn sculpture. A third man stood almost directly between Bolan and the safety of the darkness beyond.

The Executioner suspected that other members of the assault team patrolled the grounds out of sight. The chances of completing an end run around the building were probably no better than punching through the middle.

Bolan levered himself over the wall and dropped silently into a flower bed, rolling with the impact. Fortunately, the crackle of flames behind him made any small noises undetectable. On the other hand, it made the warrior more vulnerable to a foe creeping up on him.

The enemy fifty yards away was still distracted by the exchange of gunfire at the far end. Bolan angled for the darkness surrounding a small gazebo in the midst of a rose garden. He ran low to the ground, trying to minimize the possibility of being silhouetted against the burning house.

When Bolan was five yards from the pavilion, a gunman holding an Uzi walked around the corner. Their eyes locked, and the Uzi swung in Bolan's direction.

The Executioner dived a fraction of a second after the gunner fired, the 9 mm slugs whistling through the air above his back. His dive terminated against the hardman's knees, and the pair fell in a tangled heap.

The other guy was hard-muscled and angry. He fought dirty, trying to knee Bolan in the groin as the two men wrestled with both hands, desperate for control of the Uzi.

Bolan rolled on top and twisted down the butt of the Uzi until it cracked sharply against the other man's head. The Executioner ripped the gun from momentarily slackened fingers and brought the butt down once again, this time with force on the hardman's temple.

He swiveled around as his peripheral vision caught a hint of movement.

Bolan and the man approaching fired simultaneously, a grouping of slugs thudding into the gazebo. The Executioner hadn't missed. The other man clutched his belly, then sank to his knees before falling on his face.

The warrior mounted the steps of the gazebo and lifted his head slightly over the railing. The two gunners from the far end had disposed of the survivor and were running toward the sounds of shots.

Bolan knew that some troops, especially proud, violent units, sometimes substituted bravery for tactics. The two gunners were charging for the gazebo, disregarding personal safety in their haste to reach the battlefield.

The Executioner popped over the railing and nailed the closer man with a hammer strike, chest high. Bolan shifted targets quickly, but the second man had already hit the ground rolling. The guy came up on one knee beside a stone bench and replied with a burst that chewed into a roof support beside Bolan's head.

The Executioner's captured Uzi stuttered, and a sustained burst played over the bench, kicking sparks into the air. Bolan shifted the angle a fraction, and the hardman dropped as slugs ventilated his heart.

The big man raced forward and quickly patted down the corpse, pocketing a pair of spare clips for the Uzi as well as a set of car keys.

As far as he could tell, he was in the middle of nowhere. Getting back to Denver might mean a very long walk without some transport. No driver in his right mind would stop to pick up a hitchhiker as shabby and grimy as Bolan was now.

He rammed a fresh clip into the Uzi and debated hunting down the rest of the attack force. He was certain that this assault was somehow linked to the mission.

If these men were part of some unknown third force, they would most likely only be soldiers. Eliminating them would injure the opposition, but not help to penetrate the layers of deception surrounding the central mystery.

Bolan hefted the Uzi and slipped into the darkness.

KARKOV, POPOVICH and two soldiers trod cautiously in single file toward the rear of the house. Popovich had insisted on taking the point, and Karkov thought it was probably because he distrusted the abilities of the others.

All had seemed to be going well. The house had been demolished, and several survivors who had ventured out had been eliminated. Although there had been sporadic gunfire from the rear of the estate, that was only to be expected.

Karkov had begun to worry when his radio connection to the corporal commanding the second team had gone dead. He had recalled the other members of his team, posted two men as a rear guard and set out to investigate the problem.

Popovich waved them to a halt while he scanned the terrain through a pair of night-vision glasses. Satisfied, he motioned the team forward.

Karkov saw immediately why his people hadn't answered—they were dead.

The captain swore graphically in English; he had been coached so well that it took a conscious effort to speak Russian. He ordered the two soldiers to examine the perimeter, although he expected that whoever had killed his men would be long gone.

He bent over one body, noticing the man's shattered temple and that his machine gun was missing. Obviously he had been surprised. Karkov swore again and kicked the body. The stupid buggers had risked the mission by getting themselves killed. Now the rest would have the additional labor of burying the bodies in some remote field. The police would start asking some unpleasant questions if the mangled remains of four local businessmen turned up at once.

Karkov reached for his walkie-talkie to call the driver of their van to come and pick up the bodies. The captain stared at the communications device as his brow knotted in anger.

The driver wasn't responding.

BOLAN EMERGED from the light brush onto the narrow road serving the estate. The glow from the fire had guided his steps around the flank of the attackers. He had car keys in his pocket. Now he merely needed to find the vehicle they belonged to.

He made his way carefully up the road, examining the tree line for signs of camouflaged cars or trucks. The panel van was nearly invisible in the intense blackness of a starless night.

The Executioner crept around the rear of the van and discovered that a sedan was parked beside it. He could hear the squeak of the driver's seat in the van and listened carefully, finally deciding that only one man had been left on guard.

Bolan edged up the side of the van until he reached the driver's door. Luck was with him—the window was open to catch the evening breeze. The warrior slammed the butt of the Uzi into the side of the driver's head, knocking him unconscious before the man even suspected he had company.

Bolan tried the keys in the ignition of the sedan and the engine coughed to life. He turned on the headlights and left the engine running while he raised the hood of the van and made sure that no one would be able to use it as a pursuit vehicle.

The warrior spent the last few moments searching the van for anything of value. He discovered little of interest other than a collection of wallets, obviously left behind by members of the team for later collection. None had wanted to risk losing them and providing any clues to investigators.

A sound strategy, but Bolan had spoiled their plan. He hoped that the information they gave up would lead somewhere other than another dead end.

15

Bolan checked the car registration and found the address of the owner, a James Tanner. Flipping through the wallets, he recognized from a photo ID that Tanner was the man he had slugged with the Uzi behind the Old Dogs' estate. He decided to make Tanner's home his first stop of the evening.

He pulled onto a rutted pathway and turned right at the first road he came to. A sign indicated that he was approaching Boulder, which was the wrong direction. He slowed the car and made a U-turn, heading back the way he'd come.

The brief tour gave the big man plenty of time to think. The element that knit together all the separate threads of his mission so far was the buying and selling of military secrets, particularly those dealing with electronic warfare. Almost any power or information broker would be willing to pay huge sums for accurate information.

The Old Dogs had made themselves rich by trading knowledge among industrialists. The Mafia had gorged itself on the fat profits to be found in the armaments industry. But who would profit from selling the U.S. armed forces defective materials? Who could profit from the destruction of the Old Dogs?

An idea screamed for attention in Bolan's mind, but he didn't much like the answer it provided.

Bolan found the address he sought in a quiet residential neighborhood. Tanner's house, a one-story ranch-style, sported a flagpole with a drooping American flag rising from the manicured lawn. Inside, the house was furnished in early Americana and Swedish modern. Nothing about the place differentiated it from any other middle-income suburban dwelling.

Bolan took the opportunity to telephone Brognola, waking the big Fed from one of his infrequent sound sleeps. Hal came fully awake as his friend related the results of his investigation.

Bolan read off the list of participants in the attack from their wallet IDs, and Brognola promised to have the names traced and get back to him in a few hours at most.

The big man continued his search. He pulled pictures from the walls, carved up cushions and mattresses with a sharp kitchen knife, pulled drawers from dressers and emptied them completely. He even unscrewed the brass bed to see if anything had been concealed within the hollow tubing and removed the light switch plates in case anything had been stashed behind them.

When he was finished, it looked as though a very wild yet methodical cyclone had struck Tanner's neat dwelling.

There wasn't a thing out of the ordinary in the whole place. The man didn't even own a gun, although he certainly had carried one tonight.

When Brognola called back, the Fed had little to report. None of the men showed up on any list that the FBI or CIA were prepared to talk about. The men weren't totally clean, most having some minor infraction on their records ranging from driving while intoxicated to unpaid parking tickets. The most serious was an arrest for assault. One of the men had nearly beaten to death a bum who had spit on him. Apart from those little nuggets, the men checked out as honest, tax-paying citizens.

There were some similarities, though, that Bolan found intriguing. Each was a businessman or salesman with a reason to travel freely. All had emigrated from scattered European countries within the past ten years. Fewer than half were married, in each case to a woman who had come to America with them.

A suspicious man might see a sinister plot in the innocent backgrounds of the men.

Bolan was the original man from Missouri. He expected the worst, and the demons seldom disappointed him.

COLONEL VALERI LYALIN gazed over his tented fingers at the shaken Karkov. Although the captain was doing his best to conceal his worry, he knew that the colonel might shoot him on the spot for such gross incompetence.

Lyalin rose from behind his desk and walked to his subdued subordinate. "Don't move one inch," he barked sharply as Karkov's eyes swiveled.

The colonel stared from his gaunt height into the eyes of his subordinate, searching for the least hint of disloyalty. Both men knew that the American intelligence authorities would welcome Karkov with open arms. If the colonel had found in Karkov's eyes even the slightest inclination to betray their organization, he would have silenced the traitor forever with the Walther P-5 weighting his pocket.

Tiny beads of sweat collected over Karkov's forehead as he withstood the senior officer's scrutiny.

The colonel nodded, satisfied. He prided himself on his ability to read a man, to detect any sign of wavering, possibly before the man had become aware of his potential for treason. The talent had proved vital to his rise to this trusted position.

Other men before Karkov had failed his private test, their only memorial being scattered bones in distant locales.

Lyalin resumed his seat behind the desk. "Tell me again how you failed so woefully," he said, easing the tension marginally.

When Karkov began to speak, a lighter tone colored his voice as he realized that he would live. The captain related how he had hastily concealed the bodies of his men in the woods. The survivors had stolen a pickup from a farm, pushing the vehicle down the long lane to avoid being spotted.

Since the police hadn't yet arrived, Karkov still had had time to load the dead men into the pickup and hide them in a disused cave that he had scouted for just such an eventuality.

The colonel hardly listened. The measures that Karkov had undertaken were adequate for the moment, but wouldn't be enough for the long haul.

Eventually his men would be reported missing by families or employers in their everyday lives, and there was the possibility that some nosy hiker might stumble on the bodies dumped in the mountain cave.

Sooner or later the entire operation would have to be abandoned. His superiors in Moscow had granted him full authority to act as necessary to preserve the security of his mission. If he allowed this failure to escalate into an international incident, their wrath would be terrible. Being reduced to a private soldier and having privileges suspended would be a minor punishment.

"Enough!" he said, cutting off Karkov in midstream. He gave rapid, concise instructions to the captain regarding the unit's departure from the area. There was little to say, since the plan had been long formulated and thoroughly prepared. Some months in the future, after minor cosmetic surgery, he and his men would have new lives and identities in another midwestern city.

The bodies should remain hidden well enough for the short time before his organization left in Denver. If the corpses were discovered in the distant future, they would simply be another unsolved mystery.

"There is one final instruction," the colonel said. "Bolan must be eliminated. He has hurt us badly. We must have our revenge and, more important, remove a very dangerous loose end."

Karkov nodded in agreement. Clearly their enemy could not be allowed to live.

"Are you and your men up to the job?" the colonel asked.

Karkov didn't hesitate before replying that he and his men were anxious to avenge their comrades.

The colonel nodded in his turn. Karkov had returned the only answer a true solider could give. "However, for the present, I want you only to locate him and report back to me, unless there's an opportunity for you to kill him with ease. Understood?"

The captain answered in the affirmative, although not pleased with his colonel's lack of faith.

Lyalin dismissed the junior officer and picked up the telephone receiver. Karkov was a good man, but his stay in America had made him soft. He doubted if the young officer and five of his men were a match for this one-man American killing machine.

A moment later he replaced the phone. Reinforcements would soon be on their way.

KARKOV GATHERED the remainder of his team, who had been waiting morbidly outside the colonel's room, ears cocked for the sound of a shot.

He filled them in on their new mission—the hunt for Mack Bolan. "How the hell are we going to find him?" one man objected. "Where do we start?"

Karkov frowned at the questions. Discipline had eroded badly since they had come to America. His men could hardly salute him if they happened to see each other on the street. It was at times of stress that they were most likely to display the very American democratic tendency to bicker over every command.

"We'll track him to Alaska, if we have to," he snapped. "But if we move quickly, we might still find him in Denver. In the morning we'll contact every informant in the city. In the meantime, I've been instructed to visit the homes of our dead comrades and ensure that nothing remains that could possibly link them to our organization. There's much to be done and little time in which to do it. So let's move out."

Several minutes later Karkov and four of his men pulled up in front of the house belonging to their dead teammate, "James Tanner." Colonel Lyalin had given the captain a spare key, but the man hesitated at the door. A strange sensation told him that danger waited behind its pine veneer.

Karkov dismissed the notion as nerves wound tight by an evening of death. He opened the door and groped for a light switch. When he flipped on the lights, he was shocked to discover that the house had been ransacked.

The captain pulled his pistol from his shoulder holster. The colonel's instruction about simple reconnaissance flashed through his mind, but Karkov chose to ignore it, knowing that not only did he want revenge, he needed to prove something to the colonel—and himself.

He motioned a couple of men around back. Fortunately it was still an hour before dawn, so there was little likelihood of their being spotted by a neighbor.

With two men backing him up, Karkov eased into the living room. A brief but thorough room-to-room search failed to turn up anything.

"Bolan," he concluded, spitting out the name like a bad taste as he snapped on the safety and holstered his pistol.

"It's too bad we missed him," Sergeant Popovich replied, scowling.

"He hasn't gone far," Karkov shot back. "He was looking for something, probably information on us. By the thoroughness of the search, it appears that he didn't find anything. He's probably rifling another place right now. Don't forget he has our wallets, so he has the addresses of every one of us."

"Then let's trail him. When we find him, I'd like to settle the score for our dead comrades."

"I have a better idea," Karkov said, "one that will ensure that we take him alive. But we have to move quickly. Marian, drive around to the other three houses and see if you can find him. Don't let yourself be spotted. The rest of you come with me."

Karkov sped off, pleased with his ingenuity.

BOLAN FOUND the contents of the second house no more informative than the first. It was nearly nine o'clock in the morning and he'd progressed no further in the investigation. The warrior was frustrated, but had to press on. The opportunity to examine the homes of the dead men could evaporate at any moment, and for the present, it was the only game in town.

The third house smelled slightly, as though cleanliness hadn't been a great priority for the owner. Piles of magazines, newspapers and assorted junk covered most surfaces. If anyone was likely to have been a little careless, this man might be the one.

The study yielded hard-earned gold. The ashtray on the desk contained wisps of crinkled ash, the remnants of a piece of paper burned among the cigarette butts. Bolan doubted that they would produce any data, but he deposited them in a plastic bag fetched from the kitchen for later examination, just in case.

A wastepaper basket beside the desk held scraps of paper ripped into fairly small chunks. Bolan gathered them up as well.

But the big prize dropped into the warrior's hands as he combed through the bookshelves. A thick dictionary folded open to reveal a hollowed-out space that contained a small notebook. A quick look revealed that Bolan had discovered a codebook. The closely printed pages were filled with columns of keywords and their meanings.

He finished rifling through the rest of the house with the same intensity he'd employed previously. If the guy had slipped up once, maybe he had committed a second error.

However, turning the place upside down revealed nothing else, so Bolan decided to move on and check out the last address. As he drove away, he didn't notice a husky man in a corner coffee shop watching him leave.

KARKOV WORE a satisfied smile. The planted codebook and phony message had been a stroke of genius on his part, a classic disinformation ploy.

The captain believed that Bolan was a smart, resourceful man, a very worthy opponent. Karkov didn't need to check the house to make sure that the big man had discovered the clues but he did anyway, just to be certain.

When Bolan arrived at the appointed time and place this evening, he wouldn't get quite the reception he expected.

Karkov was looking forward to the meeting.

The captain thought again about telling Colonel Lyalin, but decided against it. Even though the codebook was due to expire in a few days, allowing it to be taken, even briefly, represented a serious breach of regulations.

With any luck, Karkov would recover it from Bolan's body, and the colonel would be none the wiser.

WHEN BOLAN FINALLY returned to his motel, he spent a challenging couple of hours assembling the scraps of paper extricated from the garbage. The final product appeared to be a routine letter referring to some shipment of industrial parts.

When he checked the message against the codebook, however, it told a different story. The dead man had been ordered to meet with a technician for a major aircraft manufacturer to obtain details of the alloys used in some highly classified experimental airplanes. The message specified the contact point and the rules to be used to signal whether the meeting was a go.

The rendezvous was planned for nine o'clock that evening in the industrial section of the city.

Bolan decided it was a meeting he'd like to attend. One of the opposition might be there to take the place of the dead man, which would give him another opportunity to zero in on exactly whom he was fighting.

At the same time he could uncover yet another leak in the defense industry.

Bolan phoned Brognola at the Justice Department to report the latest developments and promised to courier the codebook back to Washington at the first opportunity.

The Fed, as distrusting a man as Bolan, was concerned about the upcoming meeting. "Dammit, Striker," Brognola griped, "it just doesn't ring true. Someone suddenly screws up on this nowhere mission to the extent of leaving a secret codebook to be found? On top of that, a crumpled note directs you to an exchange that takes place this very evening. It stinks."

"Not to worry, Hal," Bolan replied. "I don't buy into the scenario, either. It just doesn't fit. You can be sure that I'll be on the lookout for a setup."

Brognola was more than likely right, Bolan thought as he hung up. There was an excellent chance that this was a clever trap baited with a lure he couldn't resist.

Bolan began to clean his weapons in preparation for the night's work. He was a wily old fish, he reflected, and had always been able to wriggle off the hook no matter how tempting the bait.

He hoped this time would be no different.

16

Bolan pressed into the shadows, the Beretta in his hand questing for a target as a tinny rattle sounded from the darkness ahead. He relaxed as two cats ran screeching across the deserted road that wound through the industrial park.

The warrior had checked out the meeting site earlier in the day. Then, the small industrial center had bustled with activity. Now the factory shifts were over and the white-collar workers had retreated to the suburbs. Only the occasional security car disturbed the silence. Yellow-orange lamps broke the blackness at wide intervals.

The warrior had donned combat black for the occasion. The Beretta, equipped with a sound suppressor, formed part of his arsenal, while the Desert Eagle Magnum tugging at his shoulder provided a powerful stopping tool. Slung over his shoulder was his main firepower—a compact Heckler & Koch MP-5 SD, the silenced version of the MP-5, with a retractable stock. Bolan carried a liberal supply of 30-round magazines for the 9 mm submachine gun.

He warily approached the first checkpoint, which was a bus shelter. According to the encoded message, if the rendezvous was a go, a blue New York Yankees baseball cap should be on a bench in the shelter. If it sat right side up, the meeting was on as scheduled. If it had been turned upside down, then the meet was moved to an alternate site an hour later. If there was a different cap, then the meeting had been aborted.

The Yankee cap rested the right way up, signaling the all clear.

The big man moved cautiously, pausing frequently to listen for sounds that would indicate that he was being followed. A steel galvanizing factory about a hundred yards ahead was the objective. If sentinels had been posted to spring a trap set for him, he should encounter them sometime soon.

Bolan scanned the rooftops and shadows. The night-vision goggles he wore gave an eerie, distorted illusion of daylight, but failed to show any hidden watchers.

A door opened across the street, a blazing beacon in the otherwise dimly lit area. Bolan hugged the shadows until he determined that it was simply a workman taking a cigarette break.

The factory loomed large a few yards distant. Bolan was conscious that every cranny was a potential hidey-hole for a gunner. A dozen men could be hiding within feet, and the warrior would be none the wiser.

A sense of danger radiated from the gray metal door beckoning to the interior of the factory. A small red X had been chalked across the cold metal, the sign that all was well for the meeting. Bolan opened the door slowly, the Heckler & Koch submachine gun ready for trouble.

A string of industrial lights shone down the center of the factory from low metal girders. To his left, bare steel lay stacked, waiting for a trip through the galvanizing process. In front of him ran a series of wide, deep containers filled with acid. The steel was dipped and cleaned there prior to a final dip in a large vat of molten aluminum at the end to Bolan's right. A number of cranes ran on a circular track to transport the bundles of girders being treated.

The smell of acid fumes from the open vats stung his eyes and burned his throat as soon as he stepped inside the door. Ordinarily, powerful fans refreshed the air. But tonight the fans were still, and the closed room had filled with noxious vapor. The lights glowed with a faintly menacing, reddish tinge through the drifting clouds of acid vapor. The molten aluminum popped occasionally in its heated trough, sounding like the bursting of large bubble-gum balloons.

Bolan stood by the door, evaluating the situation. On the far side at the rear of the shop, a light burned in an office. Voices emanated from there, apparently in heated conversation, although pitched too low for the big man to pick out anything but an angry tone.

In order to reach the office, he'd have to cross a large open area that held piles of girders, both galvanized and raw steel. None of them stood high enough to offer adequate cover. The warrior searched for a less exposed route to the office. He decided that the forest of roof supports that carried the crane would be ideal.

He took a position between the towering acid vats under the crane hoise and extracted a small grappling hook from one of the many slit pockets of his black suit. He whirled the device above his head, aimed carefully and let it fly. The hook clinked among the steel beams, and a strong tug showed that it had found a secure purchase.

Bolan shouldered the SMG and began to climb hand-over-hand toward the ceiling. When he reached the level of the top of the acid vat, his combat senses kicked in as he experienced the feeling of being watched. He quickly released his grip and dropped six feet to the ground, rolling into the shelter of the nearest vat.

As he fell, gunshots resounded from among the ceiling supports, where the enemy lay hidden. Slugs whined as they ricocheted from metal surfaces, occasionally raising a brief spark. One round found a weak point in the vat and started a leak. Sulfuric acid poured onto the concrete floor in a steady stream.

From the direction of the firing, which was concentrated at the far end of the factory, Bolan realized that if he had continued on toward the office on ground level he would have been at the mercy of the hidden killers. By planning to travel the high road he had disrupted their carefully prepared trap. Now the opposition was improvising, a dangerous tactic without excellent coordination.

The Executioner lay low under cover, watching the door he had entered. He doubted that the exit had been left unguarded so that he could simply stroll out.

A moment later the door banged open, and someone thrust a jacket through the opening. The warrior wasn't fooled for an instant by the simple ruse, even in the poor lighting.

He focused the submachine gun on the opening, ignoring the vicious patter of slugs around him. One guy barged through the doorway at a run, while a partner provided covering fire from behind.

The Executioner caught the hardman in midstride, running a line of manglers up his side. The run ended in a stumbling, unnatural dive into the spreading pool of acid, which began to take its harsh toll immediately.

First blood to the Executioner.

Bolan waited, weapon leveled, in case the other man decided to take his chances as well. But whoever remained outside wisely turned thumbs down on a frontal rush.

The warrior decided to change position to confuse his assailants. If he waited for them to come to him, he ran the risk of being surrounded while distracted or pinned by other elements of the enemy force.

The classic strategy was to pin your opponent and then go for a flank envelopment. Bolan checked the immediate surroundings, placing himself in the enemy's shoes to the extent he could without knowing more about their strength or dispositions.

He dodged the gunfire as he broke for the front of the building. If he was planning tactics for the enemy, he would be sending men flitting over the girders to come around behind him. The warrior intended to make sure that strategy backfired.

Through the swirling fumes the Executioner saw a figure on the girders above. He skidded to a halt and fired a burst at the indistinct target.

He was rewarded with a muffled shriek as lead bit into flesh. An Uzi clattered to the concrete. The killer fell onto the edge of an acid vat, then slipped into the steaming liquid. Bolan noticed as the gunner fell that he wore a gas mask. A final bubbling yell was choked off abruptly as the wounded man vanished under the acid bath.

Bolan inserted a fresh clip in the Heckler & Koch and swung around, questing for targets running through the rafters. But he heard nothing. The sudden silence was broken only by the bubbling of the molten aluminum. The gunmen apparently had decided to let the Executioner come to them.

He would be happy to oblige.

Bolan ran back along the series of vats, crouching until he reached the last one. Beyond lay the stacks of girders awaiting treatment. He noticed that voices still murmured in the office, obviously a tape concocted for his benefit.

Bolan fired at random into the upper reaches of the factory. The fumes were so thick above that it was impossible to see the roof of the building, so he could only shoot blind.

Lead spit back at him from two different locations. The warrior noted the spots as he shifted his firing position to behind a forklift.

The Heckler & Koch kicked again, and one of the hardmen dropped headfirst to the concrete like a bagged pigeon. Receding footsteps sounded in the murk as the last assailant scrambled for safety.

Bolan smiled, grimly, since he held the advantage. Now that the ambush had failed, the lone survivor was left with the difficult task of extricating himself from a position without a clear escape route. In his over-confidence, the bushwhacker had failed to provide for a secure line of retreat.

Bolan followed the sounds of flight cautiously, aware that a cornered rat could turn viciously and fight for its life.

A heavy thump from the direction of the office indicated that the man had jumped onto the roof of the structure. Bolan sank behind a pile of galvanized piping and drew the Beretta from its custom leather. He wanted a prisoner, and he was far more likely to get one with a single precise shot than with a scattered burst from the powerful SMG.

A second loud thump followed before a big, dark-haired man poked his way around the edge of the doorway to the office. He had to have climbed through a trapdoor in the office ceiling.

The intruder saw Bolan and snapped a burst from his Uzi, the bullets going wide and smashing into the aluminum-coated pipes.

The Executioner sighted carefully and squeezed. The hardman's legs buckled, and he collapsed to the floor.

Bolan ran forward and looked warily around the corner. The gunner lay stunned or dead, a bright red mark staining his right thigh. Blood oozed slowly from the wound. The warrior checked the man's pulse and was relieved to find him simply unconscious from his fall onto the concrete floor. On closer examination, Bolan noted that he had caught the fellow in the fleshy part of the leg, painful but not serious.

The Executioner first bound the wound with a makeshift bandage, then tied the man's limbs with a light nylon rope he'd brought for just such a purpose. He cast an eye behind him occasionally, in case the man who had tried to enter the warehouse earlier put in another appearance. However, it was more likely that the guy had shown the better part of valor and got out while he could.

The gunner came too. "We're going to play a little game," Bolan began without preamble. "It's called truth or consequences. Who sent you here?"

The other man simply stared as though he didn't comprehend English.

Bolan shrugged and jerked his thumb at a nearby container. "If I remember my chemistry correctly, the melting point of aluminum is about 700 degrees centigrade. That could give a man a nasty burn, don't you think? It sure is hot in here. Are you ready to answer a few questions? Or would you prefer to go for a little dip in that vat over there, an inch at a time?"

The warrior paused for a reply. When none was forthcoming, he bent over as if to lift up his captive. "Okay, you made the choice."

"No, wait!" the man shouted. "I'll tell you what you want to know."

The man began to talk. In a short while, Bolan learned that he had captured Yuri Karkov, a captain in the KGB, one of a ring of industrial spies operating in the Midwest.

Suddenly the entire scenario became clear. Tony D'Angelo had been working with Clarkson and the Old Dogs to obtain classified information, which he then passed along to the Russians at a hefty price. He had been able to make money from every direction, including selling out his country.

When Bolan turned up in Denver after D'Angelo's death, the Russians had been panicked into taking action against the Old Dogs, not knowing if the trail leading to their operation might suddenly unravel and leave them exposed to the scrutiny of the FBI or CIA.

"One thing still puzzles me," Bolan probed. "Why were Clarkson employees being asked to pass false test data along to the Pentagon? What purpose could that serve?"

"Simple enough," Karkov answered. "If we could muddy the waters of American weapons development plans, so much the better. Anything that held you back was a benefit to us, since the technological edge is the only thing that keeps NATO ahead of the Warsaw Pact forces. In particular, it would have been a tremendous bonus if we could have sabotaged one of the space shuttles. That would have crippled your space program, perhaps permanently."

Bolan nodded in agreement. How the Russians must have valued the ruthless D'Angelo, a sociopath without a conscience, an arch-traitor as well as a criminal mastermind. The opportunity to sabotage United States interests was a bonus that would have been too tempting to ignore, particularly given the ease with which the Mob boss could execute the damage.

"All right," Bolan said, making a sudden decision. "I'm going to return you to your commander personally, because you're going to deliver a message to him from me. This has actually been a big misunderstanding, since I'm actually happy to help him. I have things to sell that he wants to buy, including technical plans for the alloys that comprise the Stealth bomber. If he wants them, I can let him have them, at the right price."

"He's hardly likely to believe you," Karkov said with expected skepticism.

Bolan pulled a sheet of paper from a pocket and stuffed it into Karkov's pocket. It contained a fictitious, though plausible, partial set of circuit diagrams for a new command helmet designed to assist fighter pilots in combat and navigation. "Listen, Karkov. I got involved in this mess because I was looking for a buyer for some merchandise that some friends have for sale. Admittedly, things have become more complicated than I had anticipated. But the deeper I got, the more I realized how much profit was to be made for the right supplier. You've lost your best source, and I'm here to pick up the slack. This is just a sample of the kind of things I can supply," Bolan bragged convincingly.

"I'm not going to carry any hard feelings just because you've tried to kill me a couple of times. If your superior doesn't think this is reason enough to meet, then he's a fool. Tell him to meet me tomorrow night with a hundred thousand dollars. That should be enough to begin negotiations. I've given him a number where he can call me to confirm.'' Bolan named a quiet meeting place outside Denver, then left Karkov tied while he went to get his car. The last of the Russian killers had vanished into the night, leaving him a clear run.

The warrior drove Karkov back to Denver and dropped him at his home. Bolan then settled into an all-night doughnut shop, his eyes watching an electronic tracker as he read yesterday's news. He couldn't be certain that Karkov had believed his story, but then what did the Russian have to lose by passing on the information to his superior? As far as Bolan was concerned, the worst that could happen would be that another attempt would be made to eliminate him. But then the big man lived with that threat every day.

A half hour later Karkov was on the move again. Bolan followed at a safe distance, led by the tiny but powerful transmitter he had buried among the folds of the bandage he had made for the Russian's leg.

Bolan expected that Captain Karkov would waste little time reporting in and seeking medical attention. This would provide one more piece of information and allow the Executioner to decide where to strike next.

The tracker indicated that Karkov had come to a halt. Bolan parked and covered the last hundred yards on foot along a quiet residential street. He was surprised to find that the zero point registered somewhere inside a small church. He didn't recognize the name of the denomination, which was hardly surprising, as the so-called church probably existed purely as a front for the Russian organization.

It presented an ideal cover, since people could come and go freely without attracting attention from local residents. No one would harbor the least suspicion that a church sheltered a nest of Soviet spies.

The big man wondered if the local commander—no doubt a good Communist—got up on Sundays and preached sermons to his flock of killers as well as any stray visitors who wandered into the church expecting a service.

Who said the KGB didn't have a sense of humor?

17

Colonel Valeri Lyalin looked carefully at the documents spread across his desk. As a trained engineer and a KGB officer, he had an appreciation of the value of the plans now in his possession.

It had been rumored that the Americans had made great advances in technology that allowed a pilot to assimilate the barrage of data necessary to fight a combat aircraft. Lyalin's KGB masters would pay almost any amount for the complete set of plans.

Provided, of course, they were genuine.

This Bolan was a fox who had bitten Lyalin every time he reached out a hand to strike him down. The colonel expected that he'd be bitten again if he was foolish enough to try to deal with the wily American. The lure of the valuable plans was tremendous, but Lyalin's nose for trouble warned him that Bolan was too unpredictable to be trusted. The colonel could never be certain if he was being led by the nose down a false trail.

The worst scenario was that Bolan intended to lure him into a position where he would be captured or killed. Grim as the possibility was, experience told the colonel to expect nothing else.

Bolan would, however, have his meeting.

"Tell, me, Karkov, how exactly did you obtain this information from Bolan?" The colonel's eyes bored across his desk into his assistant, challenging him to answer.

The captain explained that Bolan had proposed the truce when only the two of them survived the ambush in the factory. Karkov had felt it was his duty to bring the documents back to his commander for assessment.

Lyalin wondered what kind of idiot his subordinate thought he must be to believe such a lame story. Never mind the fact that the captain had contradicted his orders by laying an unauthorized ambush for the American—although he could have forgiven that if it had been successful.

"Is that so, Captain?" the colonel asked coldly. "Or was it that he captured you and you begged for mercy by telling him everything you knew and by offering to turn informer?"

"Not at all! I assure you, Colonel, that nothing transpired that would compromise our operation. I am not a traitor." Panic wavered at the edge of Karkov's voice.

"That is very good, Comrade." Lyalin pushed back his chair and moved away from his desk. "I very much dislike traitors." With that final pronouncement, the colonel pulled his FN 9 mm compact pistol from his pocket and fired a point-blank shot into Karkov's head.

Colonel Lyalin then moved past the body and left the room to use the telephone in the adjoining office.

As he dialed Bolan's number, he called for his orderly to clean up the debris in his office.

Karkov had made a terrible mess of his desk.

BOLAN REPLACED the receiver, satisfied with the call. The Russian had changed the time and place of the meet and had specified various security conditions, including that neither party be armed and that both come alone. But none of these precautions had come as a surprise. It was all part of the game.

The warrior had no intention of venturing out unarmed, nor did he expect Lyalin to do so. In fact, the Russian would probably violate every one of his own rules.

Bolan had come to expect double-dealing and betrayal as a matter of course, and he felt sure that the Russian wouldn't change his spots on this occasion.

The meet had been moved up to early evening and the place changed to a suburban housing development. Presumably Lyalin had made the change almost at random, both to foul up any preparations Bolan might have made and to assert a small amount of control. Bolan was inclined to play along if small compromises were the only way to entice the Russian into his gunsights.

An hour and a half before the Executioner was to depart, Lyalin called and changed the meeting place once again, this time to a lightly wooded area outside of town. He also bumped up the time by an hour, which meant that Bolan had to leave immediately.

The last-minute change served the enemy well. If Bolan had prepared a trap, the sudden change would have destroyed any arrangements he might have made.

Bolan suspected that he was being led to a site that the Russian had had in mind all along. Whoever chose the battleground had a significant advantage, particularly when the other party had to charge blind. Despite this, Bolan wasn't concerned. He'd been through this kind of exercise many times before, and had always managed to stay alive.

He turned over possible scenarios in his mind during the drive to the meeting ground, planning how he would deal with each eventuality. He was armed with the same three weapons he had used during the factory battle the night before. He figured they would serve him well again today.

The warrior turned his vehicle through a broken and rusting gate and down a rutted lane that led into a meadow. Scattered trees provided limited cover among the long grass and wildflowers. The light had already started to fade as the sun sank in an orange haze of clouds behind the high Rocky Mountain peaks to the west.

Bolan scanned the placid terrain for signs of ambushers crouched behind the surrounding greenery, but nothing caught his eye other than a black limousine parked a half mile away.

The Russian had chosen the site well, since it would be impossible to approach his position in any strength without being spotted. The only weakness he could see was the absence of an obvious line of retreat. Either

Lyalin didn't expect to need one, or there was another way out not immediately apparent to Bolan.

He stopped the car and raised a pair of 7×50 binoculars for a closer examination of the battleground. He scanned every inch, but couldn't discern anything out of the ordinary. Even the limousine showed no signs of life. Thus far it seemed that the KGB colonel was following to the letter the procedures they had agreed upon.

For a moment Bolan wondered if the KGB had actually taken the bait completely and expected him to provide military secrets in return for money. Brognola had provided him with a set of diagrams that to a nonexpert in the field appeared totally convincing. If he had suckered in the Russians, should he turn them over to the FBI to string along and exploit?

The warrior rejected the idea. Playing the role of a mercenary information dealer didn't appeal to him over the long run. The Executioner preferred more direct, more permanent solutions that removed the threat once and for all, the kind that resulted in a funeral and a headstone.

He eased the car into motion and continued down the narrow trail. A hundred yards from the limo he noticed from the corner of his eye a brief flash to his left. It could have been the gleam of sunlight on a discarded bottle—or on a gun barrel.

The warrior wasn't about to take any chances. He gunned the big car, aiming straight for the limo. A moment later he jerked open the door and rolled onto the ground.

The limo leaped into motion, reversing out of the path of the big Oldsmobile, which began to slow as soon as Bolan's foot left the accelerator.

Bullets thudded into the Olds's bodywork as guns chattered from both sides of the road. From the sound of the reports, Bolan guessed that the enemy was firing that old Russian favorite, the AK-47 assault rifle.

The limo retreated farther out of range until it vanished among a row of distant trees.

Bolan was fully occupied with the remaining troops. There appeared to be three separate firing positions, forming a triangle. Two were situated on the far side of the track, while the third lay directly ahead. Bullets chewed into the soft earth around Bolan and nipped blades of grass near his head.

The warrior lay crouched in a depression by the side of the pathway, but he couldn't remain there much longer. Either a stray bullet would core him as he hugged the dirt, or one of the opposing gunners would creep up and eliminate him. He was on the defensive, and he didn't like it.

The numbers were counting down to destruction for one side or the other. The enemy had all the advantages in manpower and position.

The only edge the Executioner held was in guts and fury.

Bolan moved fast, rolling up and out of the depression, leaping to his feet and into a zigzag sprint. He dived to the ground a few yards away, taking cover behind a fallen and decaying log. A tree stump provided partial protection from the killers behind him.

Enemy gunfire kicked wood chips from his shelter as he aimed the Heckler & Koch for the single gunman in the woods ahead. He steadied the SMG in a notch and fired rapid, controlled bursts at the muzzle-flash of the AK-47.

The Executioner had almost drained the magazine of the stubby grease gun before one of his 9 mm missiles hit home. The Russian hardman flopped forward from behind his tree and crumpled in plain sight.

Bolan immediately shifted his attention to his rear. One gunman had remained in position, snapping sporadic bursts that whistled around Bolan's meager hideout. The other Russian had apparently disappeared—no doubt he was working his way closer to Bolan's position.

The warrior scanned the vicinity, paying particular attention to the ground to the east, which had already faded into gloom with the imminent fall of night. A modest breeze blew, shaking the long grass and making it difficult to detect sound or movement. He used the brief pause to insert a fresh clip in his weapon.

A flicker of movement caught his attention as a darker shape showed itself against the indigo sky. Bolan watched the spot for a moment and was rewarded as the outline of a black-clad back showed fractionally above the level of the waving grass.

The Executioner's gaze followed the rapidly moving figure that slithered toward his flank and he gently squeezed the trigger of the H & K subgun. A trio of 9 mm rounds flew across the meadow, stitching three precise holes along the Russian's spine.

Now it was down to a one-on-one contest between Bolan and the surviving Russian assassin. The warrior held the advantage, since the other man was alone after having started out as part of an assault team. That fact was bound to unnerve the lone gunman.

Bolan intended to use this psychological advantage to full effect. He broke cover and angled toward the clump of trees where the gunner lay hidden, firing from the hip as he ran and dodged.

Suddenly a strange sound burst from the distance, breaking his stride. Bolan hugged the ground until he identified the noise as the growl of a powerful motorcycle engine.

At that moment, the machine burst from the tree line, speeding in the Executioner's direction. The Russian drove at less than full throttle over the bumpy ground, with one hand on the handlebars and the other ready to trigger his side arm.

Bolan stayed cool as the biker aimed for his position, firing short bursts as he approached. The warrior recognized this as a desperate maneuver, and drew the mobile gunman forward into point-blank range. Bolan had little fear of being hit by a shot from the unstable, bouncing gun.

When the motorcycle was only thirty yards away, the Executioner raised himself and opened fire. His first burst tore into the biker's chest, sending the man tumbling over the back wheel as he and the bike parted company. The vehicle reared on one wheel and toppled, kicking up a fountain of dirt as it fell.

The occupants of the limousine had decided that the situation had deteriorated from bad to disastrous. The stretched car accelerated down the lane.

Bolan fired his weapon as soon as the limo came into range, but the bullets bounced away, indicating that reinforced armor lay beneath the bodywork. It hurtled on, accelerating as it ran the gauntlet, as unstoppable as a charging elephant.

The warrior drew the Desert Eagle. If any of his weapons could cause damage to the limo, it would be the big .44 Magnum.

The Executioner sighted down the ten-inch barrel at the oncoming vehicle and squeezed off several rounds, aiming for the driver. Holes appeared in the windshield but the man apparently led a charmed life, for he continued to steer unimpeded. The limo whizzed by, leaving Bolan shooting at its rear. A few more shots at the tires missed their mark, and then the big car was beyond effective range.

Bolan tried to start his Oldsmobile, but a stray bullet had evidently nicked something vital. He ran to the downed motorcycle. The big machine, a Goldwing, appeared undamaged. It started cleanly, and the warrior streaked in pursuit of the limousine.

He followed the highway back to town, reasoning that Colonel Lyalin would make for the safety of his base, possibly believing that it hadn't yet been discovered.

Bolan drove the motorcycle hard along the mountain highway, although aware that a false move might send him crashing over a cliff to a painful end a few hundred feet below.

In minutes the taillights of the limo appeared ahead. He eased up on the throttle slightly as he gained ground on the speeding car, waiting for a straightaway where he could use a free hand to fire the submachine gun, which had been slung over his shoulder.

A sharp bend loomed ahead, and Bolan leaned into the turn, guiding the Goldwing smoothly with an experienced hand. Less than one hundred yards separated the two vehicles.

As Bolan came out of the turn, a stream of black oil shot from the rear of the limousine onto the highway. He swerved to avoid it, but half a second later, his bike hit the slick and skidded out of control.

Bolan fought the machine, but it had a life of its own and headed straight for the edge of the cliff.

There wasn't a damn thing he could do about it.

The Goldwing smashed into the guardrail, the impact hurtling Bolan through the air toward the ground—five hundred feet below.

It would be a hard landing.

18

Colonel Lyalin gloated with pleasure as he saw Bolan plunge over the cliff. His mission was in tatters and his career possibly ruined because of the interference of the American, but at least he had enjoyed a final revenge.

The sting of any future punishment would be lessened by his elimination of this American who had proved to be the deadliest and most persistent enemy the Russian had ever confronted.

Now he must go back and face the laborious task of removing all traces of the local operation prior to relocating a little farther east. A damned nuisance, but one that Bolan had made necessary.

Lyalin allowed himself a stiff drink of good Russian vodka from the back seat bar. A toast to the late American fighter.

LYALIN'S REJOICING was premature, for Bolan was still alive. The short, airborne trip had ended in the leafy embrace of a tree that clung to the side of the cliff some fifty feet from the top.

Apart from an ache in one shoulder and a few scrapes, he had escaped uninjured. His submachine gun had disappeared, but he still carried the Beretta and Desert Eagle.

He struggled up the rocky cliff, making sure of each foothold, aided by tough mountain plants. When he edged over the top he headed immediately for the motorcycle. The front wheel was bent beyond repair, the handlebars were twisted and the engine looked as though it had been beaten with a hammer.

Since there was no alternative, Bolan started to walk. He heard a vehicle draw near, and a few minutes later a pickup slowed beside him. Bolan was careful to keep his weapons out of sight.

"Is that your bike back there?" the driver asked. "Looks like you took a nasty spill."

Bolan nodded.

"If you want a lift into Denver, hop in the back."

The big man didn't need coaxing and climbed in. From the smell, he guessed that the last passengers had been hogs. After a bumpy and uncomfortable trip, the Good Samaritan dropped Bolan on the outskirts of town.

The warrior needed a set of wheels to continue the journey, and walking through the front door of a rental agency was out of the question. Accepting a ride in the back of a pickup was one thing. Strolling through the door of a place of business togged in a blacksuit and toting weapons was quite another. He'd have to hot-wire a vehicle and have Brognola square things with the owner. He chose a nondescript sedan of American manufacture. No need to mess around with one of those high-tech foreign autos. A few minutes later Bolan was on his way to the KGB leader's base.

Lights glowed from the basement of the church where Lyalin and his cohorts had retreated.

Bolan checked his guns once more, making sure that he had full clips in both the Beretta and the Desert Eagle. He threaded a sound suppressor onto the barrel of the Beretta, hoping to retain surprise for as long as possible.

The Executioner stood by a rear door leading into the church hall, deliberating on the best method of attack. A station wagon stood nearby, partially filled with boxes of papers and assorted office supplies. There was no sign of the battle-scarred limo. Presumably Lyalin didn't care to go driving around the country in a conspicuous bullet-riddled limousine. He'd have enough problems without attracting unwanted attention from the police.

Bolan's thoughts were brought to an abrupt end as the door swung wide and a man emerged carrying a box. As soon as the Russian saw the big man, he dropped his load and reached for the gun nestled in a shoulder holster.

The Executioner fired first, sending a 3-round burst straight through the Russian's heart.

Bolan plunged through the open doorway and down the stairs to the basement. At the bottom of the steps was a large open area partially filled with filing cabinets and office equipment. Three men were packing and sorting through files. One man tended a shredder and was throwing the strips of paper it produced into an incinerator for good measure.

"Everybody on the floor!" Bolan shouted.

The man by the shredder ducked out of sight. Distracted by the sudden movement, Bolan shifted his attention momentarily, and the other two dived for the floor, reaching for their guns.

Bolan slid behind a filing cabinet and targeted the man behind the shredder, who was now holding a Browning pistol in his hand. The Executioner fired once and lodged a 9 mm parabellum in the man's temple.

He shifted targets quickly. The other two were firing from behind overturned tables. The one with a mini-Uzi was peppering Bolan's position with a steady stream of lead.

Under good conditions and adequate light, the Executioner had few equals in marksmanship. He wasted no time in proving it.

Selecting the 3-round burst mode, he targeted the guy with the Uzi. He looked around the filing cabinet and sighted down the barrel. Bolan rode out the recoil as the bullets left the weapon in quick succession and drilled the gunner.

As his companion sank out of sight, blood pumping weakly from his shattered throat, the last gunman got in a lucky shot that smashed into the barrel of the Beretta.

Bolan dropped the gun, his hand burning from the impact. He drew the Desert Eagle with his left hand as he flexed his injured right.

The Russian, emboldened by his success, rushed forward to finish Bolan off. Instead he ran right into the sights of the big .44.

The Executioner blew away the Russian's surprise with two rapid shots at point-blank range, the powerful slugs ripping the guy's chest into pulped flesh and splintered bone.

The Russian fell, dead before he hit the floor.

Bolan guessed that only one target still remained. He had eliminated all of the Russian pawns. Now it was time to checkmate the king.

The warrior hunted cautiously, knowing that Lyalin would be a dangerous and devious opponent.

He cracked open a door that led to an inner sanctum and eyeballed the interior through the opening. There were only a few places for the colonel to hide: under the desk, behind the door or out of sight in a corner. But Bolan couldn't detect even a hint of the enemy in any of the obvious places. All the windows were sealed, and he didn't see any other doorways.

A suspicion crept over him. To test his theory, he picked up the body slumped by the shredder and tossed it through the doorway.

Shots rained down on the corpse. Somehow Lyalin had managed to perch above the door, where he'd have been able to ambush Bolan as soon as he stuck his head into the room.

The Executioner angled the Desert Eagle around the edge of the door and fired a shot, blind.

Lyalin realized that he was in a losing battle. He couldn't maintain his precarious hold forever, and as soon as he lost his balance, he'd fall right into Bolan's field of fire.

The colonel tossed down his pistol. "Don't shoot," he called out. "I'm surrendering to you." He followed his words immediately by jumping to the carpeted floor, landing rather heavily.

Bolan regarded his enemy with interest; Lyalin did the same. "So we finally meet," the KGB colonel said. "It's an honor to lose to such a worthy opponent. However, would you help me to my feet? I think I may have broken my ankle."

"Sorry, Lyalin. You've managed just fine this far."

The man shrugged. "You're right. I'll just have to take care of myself." He propped himself up on both hands, grunting with the effort.

Pointed steel suddenly filled his hand, and his arm flashed back to throw the knife he had palmed.

The Executioner fired at point-blank range, the .44 Magnum slug carving its way through Lyalin's brain.

The last double cross had backfired.

**A treacherous tale of time travel
in a desperate new world.**

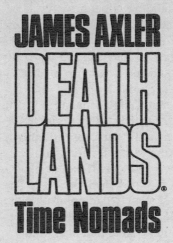

JAMES AXLER
DEATH LANDS®
Time Nomads

Trekking through the blasted heart of the new America, Ryan Cawdor and his band search the redoubts for hidden caches of food, weapons and technology — the legacy of a preholocaust society.

Near death after ingesting bacteria-ridden food, Ryan Cawdor lies motionless, his body paralyzed by the poison coursing through his system. Yet his mind races back to the early days in the Deathlands…where the past is a dream and the future is a nightmare.

You don't know what NONSTOP HIGH-VOLTAGE ACTION is until you've read your 4 FREE GOLD EAGLE® NOVELS

Do you know a real hero?

At Gold Eagle Books we know that heroes are not just fictional. Everyday someone somewhere is performing a selfless task, risking his or her own life without expectation of reward.

Gold Eagle would like to recognize America's local heroes by publishing their stories. If you know a true to life hero (that person might even be you) we'd like to hear about him or her. In 150-200 words tell us about a heroic deed you witnessed or experienced. Once a month, we'll select a local hero and award him or her with national recognition by printing his or her story on the inside back cover of THE EXECUTIONER series, and the ABLE TEAM, PHOENIX FORCE and/or VIETNAM: GROUND ZERO series.

Send your name, address, zip or postal code, along with your story of 150-200 words (and a photograph of the hero if possible), and mail to:

 LOCAL HEROES AWARD
Gold Eagle Books
225 Duncan Mill Road
Don Mills, Ontario
M3B 3K9
Canada

The following rules apply: All stories and photographs submitted to Gold Eagle Books, published or not, become the property of Gold Eagle and cannot be returned. Submissions are subject to verification by local media before publication can occur. Not all stories will be published and photographs may or may not be used. Gold Eagle reserves the right to reprint an earlier LOCAL HEROES AWARD in the event that a verified hero cannot be found. Permission by the featured hero must be granted in writing to Gold Eagle Books prior to publication. Submit entries by December 31, 1990.

HERO-1R